I0623121

LOST

TT KOVE

ARCTIC CIRCLE PRESS

PROLOGUE

*T*he police car and fire truck parked in front of our house should've given me a warning that something wasn't right. But I didn't pay them any notice as I walked down the street, headphones on, music blaring in my ears.

Only when I walked into our driveway, and turned my head for one last glance back did I glimpse a wrecked car. The police and firemen stood by it in conversation. I hurried up the steps. Only when I was in the hallway did I turn the music off.

Claws scuttled against the floor, and a moment later my puppy was in my arms, licking my face and whining.

"What's the matter, girl?" I picked her up and

headed further into the house. She squirmed in my arms.

There was a draft coming in from the veranda door. It was wide open.

"Josh?" I headed over to see if he was home, but there was no one out in the garden. "You been out alone?" I looked down at Storm, whose tongue lolled out of her mouth.

I closed the door and locked it for good measure.

"Josh?" He was supposed to be home. He was supposed to be watching Storm. Yet he was nowhere to be seen. The veranda door had been open, she could've run off—

Someone was lying on the kitchen floor.

I saw a pale hand from where I was standing.

My chest squeezed, my heart beat faster. "Josh?"

I held Storm tight—something she wasn't too happy about, but I didn't care—as I inched closer to the kitchen. The hand was attached to an arm, the arm a torso, a head—and *blood*. So much blood.

No! I turned and ran for the front door, hoping the police and the firemen were still there.

They were.

"Help!" I shouted, stumbling down the steps. They turned towards me, alarmed. "Help!" I pointed inside, lost for words. "Josh—he's—*blood*!"

For a second all was silence, frozen—and then

they reacted. I heard their voices, but my gaze had fallen on something behind them. The fire engine had moved since I'd entered the house and now I saw what was behind it and the wrecked car.

It was *another* wrecked car.

It was my parents' car—and they weren't inside it.

"No." It couldn't be. They were at work. They *should've* been at work. What was their car doing there? Why was it a wreck?

As the police officers hurried past me, I still stared at the car. I knew what it meant. What else *could* it mean?

I was frozen, clamped off, shielded somehow. I knew what this must mean, but it didn't *mean* anything. I didn't *feel* anything.

I was empty.

his was a mistake.

I'd known it before going out, but if my sister put her mind to something, she could be quite the force. So now I sat here, in a corner all by myself, since I didn't know any of Mathilda's friends. Mathilda herself had abandoned me.

There was only lager to be had, too, and I *hated* lager.

If I was going to drink in the first place, I wanted something stronger, but it seemed all of Mathilda's friends preferred the nastiness that was lager.

"Here." A bottle was thrust in front of me.

I blinked in surprise, then looked from the bottle to the person offering it. He was my age, with a long, slim body encased in skinny jeans and a thin vest.

His arms were toned, and an obscure, black tattoo covered one of his shoulders. He also wore bracelets of all kinds of colours around his wrists and a simple necklace from which a faux razorblade dangled. Another tattoo adorned his collarbone, but the vest covered it so I couldn't read what it said.

He was also wearing a pair of those big, black-framed glasses that were in right now, and behind them were bright blue eyes covered in black eyeliner. Dark hair, at least the fringe I could see, as the rest was covered by a black cap. His ears were pierced all the way up the cartilage, both of them.

"You look a little lonely." He grinned, waving the bottle in front of my face. "Can't have that, now can we?"

I blinked again, surprised at so suddenly being spoken to when I'd been ignored for the better part of two hours. Not to mention being spoken to by someone as gorgeous as he was. He could very well challenge my mate Adam for best-looks-of-the-year.

I grabbed the offered bottle and took a long sip. I couldn't tell what it was, but it burned going down, so it had to be something strong. "Cheers, mate." I took another sip for good measure, before handing it back.

"I'm Caesar." He sat down next to me on the sofa and held out his hand.

"Matt." I shook it. His handshake was firm and cool, and his hand lingered a little longer in mine than strictly necessary. I didn't mind.

"You're Mathilda's brother?" He took his own sip of the bottle, his Adam's apple bobbing as he swallowed.

"You know Mathilda?" I instinctually swept the room for her again. I'd never known she'd had such a bloody gorgeous mate.

"Nah," he denied. "A friend of hers used to be *my* best mate." He shrugged nonchalantly, but I thought I detected a story behind it. Not that I was going to push, seeing as I didn't even know the bloke.

Besides, I wanted to get pissed and forget everything for a little while.

The promise of alcohol had been the only reason I'd given in to Mathilda.

I sighed as I looked around. We were in someone's home, but I had no idea who actually owned the flat. The lights were dimmed, so it was hard to see people properly, and the air was heavy with music and smoke and the smell of beer.

"This is really dull," Caesar proclaimed. "You want to get out of here?"

My gaze slid over to him. *Why not?* It would certainly beat going back home to my bed. Here I had the prospect of more alcohol and a bloke who seemed pretty interesting. Not to mention interested in *me*. "Yeah, lets."

Caesar grinned as he stood. He offered me the bottle again, and I drank eagerly as I, too, stood. "So where're we going?"

"I was thinking my flat." He took the bottle back and ran the tip of his tongue over it, smirking as he did so.

Why not. I might as well take it out all the way.

"WANT TO WATCH PORN?"

I flopped down on Caesar's sofa, feeling rather comfortable and tipsy. We'd finished his bottle on our way, which was half an hour's walk from the flat party we'd been at.

"Sure."

"I have a subscription to this brilliant site." I couldn't see Caesar from my position, but judging by the clicking of keys, he was at the stationary Mac I'd seen when I'd entered. "It's British and the blokes are our age."

"Nice. You got something else to drink?"

"Just a second." He drew the words out slowly as his fingers kept clicking on the keyboard, then he walked over to turn on the big flat-screen telly. He skipped through channels, and then his desktop showed up on the big screen. He headed back to the Mac and I heard more clicking only now I could actually see what he was doing. A folder opened, containing videos sorted by numbers. "We'll start at number one and work our way through." With that, I heard his steps walk away.

I watched the telly as I listened to the sounds of something clinking. He'd turned the video on full-screen and two blokes, one blond, one dark-haired, started kissing on-screen.

"Vodka and lemonade. Half and half." He dropped down next to me and handed one of the two glasses over.

I took a sip and couldn't quite keep the cough back as it burned down my throat. "Half and half, all right."

"The best way to mix a drink." He clinked our glasses together before taking his own, long gulp. He sank further down on the sofa and stretched his feet, legs spread wide. "You *are* gay, right?" He cast me a quick look.

"Yeah." I'd never admitted it out loud before, but there was no reason to deny it now. I hadn't come over here to be in denial. "Totally gay."

He grinned widely, them emptied the rest of his glass in one swift gulp.

I raised my eyebrows, but he just kept on smiling.

He leapt over the back of the sofa and came back with the Vodka and the lemonade, then set to mixing himself another half-and-half.

My focus was drawn back to the telly, where the blokes had taken most of their clothes off, and were left in only their underwear and socks. They were kissing, with lots of tongue, and rubbing against each other. Both their hard dicks tented their pants.

My own cock responded to the visuals and to the small sounds escaping them between the kisses. I moved, a bit uncomfortable now, and slid further down on the sofa as well.

"So, Matty, you have a boyfriend?" Caesar kept his eyes on the telly as he asked, glass to his lips and his tongue playing over the edge of it. He had a tongue piercing, just like my friend Adam, I noticed. My cock literally twitched.

"No." I would like to have one. A certain some-one, but Adam wasn't interested in me. "I'm not really out to anyone." Only to Adam, but he saw me as a friend. Besides, he had a boyfriend.

"Why not?"

"I don't know." I sighed. "Most of the people I know are gay. It's not like anyone would have a problem with it."

He chuckled, deep in his throat, but didn't comment.

On the telly, the underwear came off and the blowjobs started. My cock swelled further in my jeans, so much so they were getting painful to wear.

I emptied the rest of my glass, then sat up to fill it up again. I didn't go quite as drastic as Caesar; I took less Vodka, more lemonade. When I sat back, I caught a dodgy movement out of the corner of my eye, and I turned my head slowly.

Caesar was rubbing himself through his jeans with one hand, while the other tilted the glass to his lips.

He must've noticed my focus was on him, because he glanced at me. "You mind?"

"No." I didn't mind at all. If Caesar wanted to wank off he was free to do so.

As I watched the two blokes on-screen suck and rub and eventually bring lube out to play, I thought maybe I'd need to wank off myself.

Caesar moved next to me and the next thing I knew, he'd unbuttoned his jeans and taken his cock out. His long fingers wrapped around it, stroking slowly up and down. His cock was big, quite above average, or at least so it seemed, and it was magnificent where it stood stiff, pointing up towards the ceiling. Foreskin covered the red, plump head every time

Caesar's strokes went up, then unveiled it again when he stroked down.

His gaze was on me again. "You want to do the honours?" He let his cock go, so quickly it slapped against his stomach, and spread his arms wide in invitation.

I licked my lips. I wanted to… and why shouldn't I? I was eighteen years old. I had no obligation to anyone. Adam… well, Adam was only my mate.

And here Caesar was… someone I didn't know, who didn't know me and what had happened in my life for the past few years. Someone who wouldn't fuck me out of pity because I'd lost a parent. Because I'd also recently lost my very best friend. Caesar, who was gorgeous and had the most magnificent cock I'd ever seen and who was so sure of himself and comfortable in his own skin.

I discarded my glass on the table and bent over to the other side of the sofa. I pushed Caesar's jeans and pants further down his thighs so I could play my fingers over his balls, then I locked my hand around the bottom of the shaft as I enveloped the plump, red, leaking head with my lips.

I hadn't given a lot of blowjobs in my life. I hadn't really done a lot of anything except a few quick BJs and hand jobs in the past year. The silky feel of the head of Caesar's cock felt divine against my tongue

—this was definitely something I could get used to doing.

If there'd been even a sliver of doubt about my sexuality, it was now blown away. Because sucking cock felt *right*.

Caesar's hand tangled in my shaggy hair. "Yeah." He groaned, moving his pelvis up and down slowly. "Just like that."

I sucked him further into my mouth, encouraged by his voice and his groans. What I couldn't reach with my mouth, I used my fist on, stroking slowly as I sucked and licked at the rest, lingering on the plump head.

From the sounds coming from the telly, I knew they'd started shagging, as their moans of pleasure could be heard loud and clear. Caesar hadn't exactly put the telly on mute and the slap of skin against skin could be heard over the sound of me sucking greedily on the stiff cock in my mouth.

Caesar's free hand travelled down my back, sliding around to my front where he swiftly unzipped my skinny jeans. A sigh of relief left me as it gave more space for my own hard cock, and then it turned into an intake of breath as his hand rubbed small, hard circles on my dick, only my boxer shorts keeping his skin from mine. The fabric of said boxers were getting damp, as I kept leaking pre-come at the attention Caesar gave me.

I pulled almost all the way off his cock, leaving only the head inside, and I ran the tip of my tongue under it.

"Oh fuck!" Caesar panted heavily. His hand slid swiftly under the hem of my boxers and I almost choked on his dick as Caesar palmed *mine*. "New plan." He tugged on my hair until I pulled off his cock with a loud, wet *pop*.

I continued stroking him, glancing up at him curiously.

His eyes were the clearest blue as he gazed down at me. "I'm going to blow you until you shoot, then I'm going to fuck you till you see stars."

His words resonated through me and I rose onto my knees as Caesar pulled me close, and straddled his spread thighs. I braced my hands on the back of the sofa and watched as Caesar sank even further down until he was on level with my cock. He grinned up at me, then swiftly sucked me in.

A loud groan escaped me at the sudden sensation enveloping my dick and I bucked my hips forward. Caesar was *bloody good* at sucking cock, that was for sure, and I felt pretty certain I would shoot soon if he kept it up. He did; he sucked me hard and fast, did the occasional deep-throat, then back to sucking.

I bent over so I could rest my forehead against the back of the sofa. My breath came in quick puffs of air. Then Caesar *stopped* sucking and instead relaxed his jaws around me, and I didn't waste any time taking the opportunity—it was like my body reacted on auto-pilot as I started thrusting into his mouth, fucking it with all I had left. My balls had drawn up tight and I was *almost... there!*

Groaning loudly, I shot inside his mouth, and then again when Caesar swallowed and sucked me clean.

He pushed against my hips, and I flopped down on the sofa on my back as I tried to get my bearings and my breathing back under control.

Caesar wiped his mouth, grinning all the while as he did so, then his hands were all over my jeans; pulling them down my hips, thighs and down my calves, until he got rid of them completely, and then they were dropped to the floor. Next he pulled off my boxers, then my socks, before he moved further up to remove my jumper and T-shirt.

I pliantly let myself be stripped naked, my gaze all the while locked on Caesar's cock, which still stood at full attention. He was going to *top* me. I nibbled on my lower lip, teeth hitting my lip piercing. I'd never bottomed before. The few sexual encounters I'd had, had been all about oral.

Caesar bent over me, still fully clothed except for his dick, which rubbed against my spent one. He kissed me, pushing his tongue into my mouth to play. I answered the kiss while my hand sought downwards, finding his cock and stroking it.

"You feel *so* good." Caesar drew back and lifted himself up so he could get rid of his vest. I ran my gaze over the flat chest revealed, taking in the hairless skin, the tattoo covering his collarbone and the ring in his belly.

Fuck! He was incredibly hot.

I continued stroking his cock, where a bead of pre-come now clung to the tip of it. I licked my lips, wanting to taste and unable to resist—so I pushed Caesar back against the sofa and leaned up and over to lick it up. The bitter taste was unusual, but not bad, and I locked my lips over the plump head again, sucking the hard dick inside my mouth, where it clearly belonged.

Groaning, Caesar arched his hips, forcing his cock deeper into my mouth. I went with it as I tried to relax my jaw as much as possible. When he went too far, I had to back off, or I'd choke and entirely ruin the good thing we had going.

I'd never been able to take my time with anyone before. The few encounters I'd had, had been quick and I'd been mostly dressed; only trousers had been pulled down to access the most vital body parts.

This however, being naked with someone and taking my time, doing actual foreplay... it was a hell of a fun time! I'd always known I *liked* cock, but I hadn't known I'd love sucking it quite so much.

Caesar eventually pushed me away with a loud moan, and he squeezed the base of his dick as he stood. "Fuck." He cursed under his voice, his eyes almost shining as they were turned towards me. "You're a pretty good cocksucker. You almost made me come there."

I sat back to watch as Caesar bent over to be rid of his jeans, boxers and socks. When he straightened again, he was gloriously naked. I licked my lips, which caused him to grin. He seemed to do that a lot.

"Be right back." He turned on his heel and walked away.

I flopped back on the sofa and moved around until I lay rather comfortably. My cock, which had woken to life again, lay half-hard against my stomach, and I stroked it lazily as I waited for Caesar to come back.

He did come back, only seconds later, with several brightly coloured condom packets, which he dropped on the coffee table along with a big bottle of lube. I felt my stomach do somersaults as my gaze went from the condoms, to the lube, to Caesar's still erect cock. *That* was going inside of me...

"What's that look for? "Caesar threw himself down on the sofa and bent forward to kiss me, his teeth nibbling softly on my piercing. "Not having second thoughts, are you?"

"No, I just, I've never—" How could I tell him I was a virgin, when Caesar was so sure of himself in everything he'd done up till now, and I most definitely weren't. I was just going with the flow —with him.

He blinked once. Twice. Realisation dawning. "You're a virgin?"

"No." I huffed, turning my head away, because *no*, I wasn't a virgin to sex—only anal sex. "Well, I've had sex before." *Kind of.* "I've just never bottomed for anyone." My voice faded out now the confession was out there.

Caesar laughed out loud, a reaction I had definitely not foreseen. He kissed me again. "Then you're in for a treat, love. Bottoming is *amazing*. Especially when I'm the one topping."

CHAPTER 2

*C*aesar sure didn't lack anything in the self-confidence department, which made me feel both safe and hot all over all at once. My cock twitched, fully hard again.

He flicked the cap of the lube bottle open and squeezed a generous amount out on his fingers. "You'll love it, trust me." He kissed me deeply, while his hand—the lubed one—ran down my arse-crack and over my hole, spreading lube all over. His index finger pressed against the tight ring of muscle and I tried my very best to relax, to not tense up, but nothing had even been inserted inside me down there, and it was *hard*. But when the muscle did give in, Caesar's finger was sucked inside me.

I had a difficult time answering the kiss as Caesar pushed deep into my arse. It didn't stop him though, he kept on kissing me regardless, and he twined our tongues together.

He spread my legs further apart with the front of his thighs, and he scooted forward until his cock nudged my arse-cheek. Another finger pushed into me, causing me to both tense and groan loudly into his mouth.

I slid my arms around his shoulders, clutching at his neck. It felt good, what he was doing to my body —it certainly wasn't like anything I'd ever felt before.

When Caesar drew back from the kiss and retracted his fingers, I lay back down properly again. I watched with heavy-lidded eyes as he reached over to the table to pick up a bright red condom packet, that he swiftly ripped open. He rolled the condom on, squeezed more lube out from the bottle, and then coated himself and me with it.

I hitched my legs up and spread them apart. I drew my bottom lip between my teeth, the piercing scraping against a tooth as I did so, but it didn't matter, because Caesar was lining up between my thighs.

He looked down at me, face for once set in a serious expression, and I gazed back, breathless. This was it; I was about to be topped, and so far, it was promising to be a really good ride.

"Ready?" He held the base of his cock and nudged the head against my lubed-up opening.

I nodded jerkily, not trusting myself to speak. I wasn't sure if I was ready, but if I wasn't now, I never would be.

Caesar leaned forward, putting pressure on his cock. My muscles resisted, but I tried my very best to relax, to give him an opening—and then he slid in. It burned; I wasn't going to lie, it burned like hell. I reached back to clutch at the edge of the sofa as my body struggled to take Caesar's considerable length.

"Shhh." He leaned forward over me, fingers tangling in my hair as he slid the rest of the way inside me. I grimaced at the burning pain as he did so and I knew I was making strangled sounds, but I couldn't stop it. He placed small kisses on my cheeks and my neck, and he kept both me and himself still to let me get used to having him buried balls-deep inside me.

I let go of the edge of the sofa and instead clutched at his neck. The burn was slowly subsiding. I felt I could breathe a little easier again. Caesar didn't look quite so sure of himself now as he watched me carefully, and I leaned up to kiss him.

"Move," I whispered, "but slow." I wasn't able to form coherent sentences. Still, it was all he needed to know.

He moved tentatively and though it still burned a little, it wasn't nearly as painful as it had been going in. I hooked my feet over his thighs, then held tight to him as he started thrusting. He went very slow at first, while watching my face for my reaction the entire time.

The burn was soon gone completely and it started feeling *good*. My eyes fluttered closed as he hit something inside, something that had pleasure shooting through my entire body. I moaned, an entirely different sound now I was finally immersed in pleasure instead of pain.

Caesar pressed his lips to mine, and I could feel him grinning. His hips started increasing in speed and he was thrusting for real. He braced his knees more solidly on the sofa, then lifted my lower body a bit as he bent further down, bending me over even more than I already was, and his hips snapped back and forth.

I knew the sounds I made were loud, but damn... from a burning pain to this kind of intense pleasure in such a short while—who would've known? I couldn't stop the moans leaving me if I'd consciously tried to. All that mattered was Caesar rocking against me, his hips driving his cock in and out, in and out, in and—

I cried out as he hit that spot again, even more perfectly this time around.

"There it is." He grunted against my ear, his hips angling so he'd nail that spot head-on on his next thrust.

"Oh fuck!"

"Now we're getting there." He wrapped his hand around my straining cock, which had deflated from the pain but were now at full erection again. He stroked me in time with his own thrust.

I didn't know what to do with myself. It was all *so much*. Almost *too* much. The cock in my arse, the hand around my dick, the warm, hard body pressing me down… I came with a shout, my whole body arching as I shot over my chest.

Caesar pulled out of me when my cock had milked itself dry, and I opened my eyes to see him ripping the condom off. He crawled over my still spread legs to straddle my hips, then he wanked himself off to completion.

I watched, mesmerised, as his semen shot over my chest, some of it even landing on my chin. When his cock was spent, Caesar let it go and instead leaned down to lap at the semen clinging to my face.

"You look good with come all over you."

That earned a startled laugh from me.

"And you felt *amazing*." He kissed my lips and I pushed my tongue out to meet him. I could taste both alcohol and his semen, and it was beyond hot.

He scooped up some of both our come on his fingers, then put them inside my mouth as he tilted his head to the side. I sucked his fingers inside, liking the taste of our mixed come.

Caesar slithered down my body and licked up all the semen he could find on his way. His cock now rested against mine—and he was still hard. "I want to fuck you again." He whispered it against my stomach, tongue poking out to dip into my bellybutton.

I could only nod. Words escaped me. I didn't have another orgasm in me right now, but I was not saying no to doing this a second time. Caesar had another orgasm in him, after all, and I couldn't deny him the chance to come again. Not when the road to climaxing was *so good*.

"Bedroom then." He jumped off the sofa with entirely too much energy. I was grabbed and hauled on my feet, then he held my glass to my lips.

I took a good sip, grateful for it as my throat was rather dry after all the moaning. He did the same, then grabbed lube, condoms and my hand and led the way into the bedroom. My gaze instantly zeroed in on his double-bed—and nothing else.

"Doggy?" He looked at me inquiringly as he bent to rip off the bedspread, throwing it carelessly to the floor.

I nodded again, crawling onto the middle of the bed as I did so. It was soft under my hands and knees. Two thick duvets and an array of pillows in all the colours of the rainbow.

Caesar came up behind me. He must've readied himself with the condom while I'd been busy getting on the bed, because he lined up at my entrance and pushed inside with ease.

I lowered my upper body to the bed and bunched my fists in the sheets. Even if I wasn't hard my body felt the sensations caused by his cock, and I found myself quite vocal again. I'd never been loud during sex before, but then I'd never bottomed before either; never felt the all-consuming desire of a big dick nudging against my prostate at each thrust.

Caesar braced his hands against my shoulders, then increased the speed of his thrusts. His balls slapped against my arse on each downward thrust, the sound mingling with my own moans.

"Yeah, yeah, yeah," he grunted.

I tilted my head slightly so I could see him. He was leaning over me, and he must've taken his cap off before getting on the bed with me, because his dark hair fell in his face now. His body was slick with sweat, his neck and face flushed, and he was *so fucking gorgeous*.

I resisted turning my face into the sheets to stifle my sounds. I wanted to watch Caesar when he came, which wouldn't be long, judging from the glazed look in his eyes.

He met my eyes then as deep, baritone groans escaped him. I knew he was coming, from the sounds, from the pleasure displayed on his face, and from the erratic thrust.

I winched as he pulled out. My arse felt like it was on fire, but it was a good kind of fire, telling me just how much pleasure I'd got from the thick cock that had caused it.

Caesar fell down on the bed next to me, and I stretched out on my stomach. He was smiling at me. "That was bloody intense." His voice was an octave deeper than normal.

"Yeah." I bit my lip. What would happen now? We'd shagged twice. Was I expected to leave? To stay? I didn't want to leave, that was for certain.

He seemed to be reading my mind. "Do you have anywhere you need to be?" When I mutely shook my head, he displayed his usual grin. "Stay, then." It wasn't even a question, but I didn't mind, because it was exactly what I wanted.

I reached out to trace Caesar's closest nipple with my index finger, then let my eyes fall shut. After the workout we'd just had, falling asleep wasn't hard at all.

CHAPTER 3

I woke to an entirely too energetic Caesar bouncing out of bed. I, in turn, groaned and rolled over to bury my face in one of the countless pillows.

"Not a morning person?" Caesar laughed at my side as he poked my side. "Come take a shower with me." When I only groaned again, he leaned down and nipped playfully at my ear. "I'll suck you off, but the offer only stands if you move your fine arse *now*." He swatted my bare arse, then laughed again as he headed out of the room.

After another groan, I finally pushed myself up. I couldn't let the chance of him blowing me pass me by, after all. So I dragged myself out of bed and trailed after him into the bathroom. He was already in the shower by the time I got there and the hot water had started to steam up the small room.

"I knew you'd come if I put it that way." He opened the glass door to smirk at me, then stepped out of the way so I could slide past him. He grabbed my cock as he closed the door again, promptly dropping to his knees.

My cock, which had been half-hard, swiftly filled up with blood as Caesar flicked his tongue out. His piercing caught my undivided attention, as I couldn't remember having felt it the night before, but I'd probably been too sloshed to take notice, what with everything else that had been new to me.

I felt it now. Oh bloody *damn* did I feel it! The metal rubbed against the head of my dick, dipped into my slit, then moved to rub over the sensitive skin right under the head. The piercing, coupled with Caesar's tongue, made my knees turn wobbly.

Bloody hell. I slid to the floor, unable to keep myself standing, and Caesar bent over so he could continue sucking my cock so expertly. His neck strained, and I put my hand there, right over the tiny little stars tattooed into his skin. They fanned over his neck and down between his shoulder blades.

I kept my gaze focused on those little stars as he worked me like a pro, like he'd never done anything but suck cock his entire life. "Fuck, Caesar." I was getting loud in my appreciations again. "I'm going to —" I grunted as I came, shooting into his waiting mouth.

Caesar licked his lips when he straightened before leaning forward to lick *my* lips. "You are by far the most delectable bloke I've ever had in my bed." A kiss followed that statement.

I snorted in amusement, not believing a word. But it was nice to hear anyway. I reached for his hard cock now. "My turn to do you."

"Nah. I've got other plans for me." He grinned and jumped to his feet, eyebrows raised as he looked back down at me. "Did I suck the ability to rise from you?"

I couldn't understand how he could be so energetic. It was entirely too early after the strenuous activities of the night before, but I did manage to push myself up on my feet, where I proceeded to position myself under the shower head. The hot water beat down on me, washing away yesterday's sweat.

His hands started soaping my back. It surprised me, but it was a pleasant surprise. I braced my hand against the wall, hoping he'd get the hint that he was free to continue doing as he pleased. He did—and I enjoyed the feel of his hands running all over my body. "How old are you, Matty?" He pushed up close to me and positioned his rock-hard cock against my arse.

"Eighteen." I pushed my arse out towards him, pressing his cock in-between my arse-cheeks. "Just so."

"Finished with your A-levels?" Wet hair was pushed from the back of my neck and soft lips ghosted over my skin. His hips rolled, rubbing his cock up my crack.

"Yeah. In uni now." I leaned against the wall, my legs shaking the tiniest bit at the teasing over my hole. "What about you?"

"Nineteen, going on twenty." He nipped softly at the thin skin on my neck, then sucked it into his mouth.

My head tilted back on a groan. "Two years older than me. Huh. I just had this notion that you were a year older, since you knew Mathilda and all." And whichever one of Mathilda's friend had previously been *his*. To that matter, talking about my sister when I was naked in the shower with another bloke—with said bloke's cock rubbing my arse teasingly—felt entirely too wrong.

"Had to repeat a year."

I didn't want to pry further into that, as I sensed it was a private matter—and I was eager to get off the subject of my sister, so I continued on. "Do you go to uni?"

"Nah. Academic life isn't for me." He licked over the skin he'd previously sucked. "I did my A-levels, but after that I was done. I work now."

"What do you do?" His cock nudged my hole and I gasped. He didn't press enough to breach, but I felt it through my whole body nonetheless.

"I'm a piercer." Lips moved down my neck and sucked on another bit of skin.

I moaned again and grabbed hold of his dark hair over my shoulder, tugging on it. It earned me a nip of teeth, which was instantly soothed by a warm, soft tongue.

The head of his cock nudged my entrance again. "I love your arse." As if to prove a point, he smacked his palm against my right cheek. "I want to fuck you again."

"You can." I angled my arse out further, my turn to nudge my hole against his head.

A nip at my earlobe, then he stepped away. "Be right back." He left me standing against the wall, padding out of the bathroom soaking wet and completely naked.

I watched him go, watched the self-confident gait as he headed off to get the necessary stuff.

I bent under the shower head again and rubbed at

my hair, pretty sure I'd got lube in it last night. Some of Caesar's shampoo helped clean it out.

He came back in when I was rinsing the shampoo out. His cock was sheathed in a condom and the big bottle of lube was held in one hand. A good portion of it was squeezed out, which he coated himself with before looking expectantly up at me.

I turned around, back to leaning against the wall. If we were going to do this, I needed to have something to lean on; if I didn't, and he started fucking me, we'd only end up in a heap on the floor.

He pressed up behind me, coating my crack with lube. I braced myself for what was next, and true enough, the head of his cock nudged against me until the tight ring of muscles gave way... and it burned as he slid inside, but more due to the fact I was sore from last night, than the fact it actually hurt to have him stretch me.

He fucked me well and good up against the wall, wringing another orgasm from me before he himself emptied into the condom with a strangled shout that might've been my name, but I was too dazed from my own climax to know for sure.

I leaned heavily against the wall as he slid out, it was the only thing keeping my trembling legs up. *I don't want to go home.*

"No one's saying you have to." He turned me around and pulled me flush up against him.

Shit. I'd said it out loud. It hadn't been my intention at *all*, but Caesar didn't seem to be freaked out over it. In fact, he seemed rather pleased.

His index finger ran over my forearm, then down my stomach to circle over my upper thigh. I didn't think much of it, just enjoyed the feel of his skin against mine.

Until he ruined the good mood with his next question.

"Why've you done this to yourself, Matty?"

CHAPTER 4

*M*y blood literally ran cold as his question and his touch reminded me of exactly what he was referring to.

I bent my head to look at where his fingers hovered over my skin—my scarred skin. Scars on both my arms and my thighs.

"I saw it last night too, but didn't want to ruin the mood." His voice was low, gentle almost. "If you don't want to answer, that's fine. I'm just curious, is all."

I swallowed heavily, unable to see anything *but* the scars now he'd drawn attention to them. I wanted to cover myself up, but his fingers were still ghosting along those on my thigh, the back of his hand *almost* touching my flaccid cock.

"I need it sometimes," I whispered, feeling I had to say *something*. We'd been having such a great time —I hoped my shame and guilt wouldn't ruin that. Then again, the sex was over, so maybe *it* was over anyway. What did I know. "To dull the pain in here." I lifted my hand, clenched it into a fist and pressed it to my chest. The other touched lightly at my temple.

"Aww, love." Caesar's arms wrapped around me in a tight hug, which startled me because it wasn't what I had been expecting.

My eyes flickered uncertainly, but he didn't say anything else, just kept on hugging me. Our naked bodies pressed up close, the hot water steaming up the room, the shower head tilted away from us.

It was weird feeling another person so close to me, and naked at that. He was all hard planes and sinewy muscles, except for the soft, flaccid cock. It was magnificent when it was erect, when it was giving me the best pleasure I'd ever felt... but it wasn't exactly bad to look at flaccid either.

It felt intimate, hugging each other close in the shower. After sex. I'd never done this before—but I bet he had. He was experienced where I was not, and he even had his own flat... I bet I wasn't the first one he'd brought over for a shag.

"You feeling a bit better?" Caesar drew back,

hand coming up to stroke my cheek as he regarded me. "I didn't mean to make you feel bad."

"You didn't." *Lie*. The reminder of my scars had made me feel bad, but having him pressed up close to me had made it a lot better. "Can I still stay?" My sentiment from earlier still stood. I still didn't want to go home.

"Well, *yeah*!" He grinned widely, then stepped backward so he could position himself under the shower head.

I watched the water beat down on him, mesmerised at the way it ran down his body. Mesmerised by his body in general. He was *fit*, he had a great personality… he could have pulled anyone, so why'd he chosen me?

"What you thinking about now?" He shook his head, splashing water everywhere. "You seem subdued again."

"Nothing." I mentally shook my head to be rid of the cynical thoughts. Here I was with a great bloke, having had great sex, and the prospect of the day ahead of us. Clearly, he'd chosen me for more than just a simple shag. Still might have been because I'd been an easy pull, sitting on my own and all, but that didn't change the fact that we *clicked*. Or at least I thought we did.

I stepped in closer to him. "Care to share some of that water? I have to wash off. *Again*."

He laughed. "Hey, I proposed showering together because of the shower sex. I'd say we accomplished what we both wanted." He splashed some of the soap he was rubbing himself in my way. "I can wash you up all nice and clean." His hands grabbed my arse, slippery fingers sliding down my crack to rub over my well-shagged hole.

I shuddered, eyes dropping closed. *Bloody hell.* I couldn't go and get turned on again. But it was good, even if he wasn't doing it to entice... well, not *merely* doing it to entice.

The water, which had lasted quite a long time, decided to *not* last for the final few minutes, so instead of hot, we found ourselves drenched in cold water.

Safe to say, we finished quickly. No more teasing touches.

Caesar handed me a towel from a cabinet, which I dried myself off with. When that was done, I tied it around my waist, because my clothes were strewn around the living room. So were his, for that matter, but he slipped into a pair of joggers and a T-shirt he had lying around.

"I'll go get *my* clothes." I felt a bit silly standing there in a towel when he was dressed.

I heard a sound—a key in the lock—but it didn't register until the door actually opened and someone stepped inside. Right in my line of sight as I headed from the bathroom towards the sofa.

"I hope you're up, love, I brought lun—" The woman broke off, wide eyes blinking as she caught sight of me. "Oh! Hello, there."

A dog trotted around her, its dark head tilting to look at me. Just as curious as its owner.

"Mum!" Caesar was in the doorway, looking like a deer caught in headlights.

For that matter, I supposed I must too. I still hadn't found my ability to speak. It was lost—along with my motor functions, because I wasn't able to move either. Until I realised I was only standing there in a towel, which also meant that my arms were on full display.

I scampered to gather my clothes, then all but ran into Caesar's bedroom to pull them on, seeing as he was still blocking the entrance to the bathroom.

I heard muffled voices, but I'd closed the door, so I couldn't make them out. Was he even out to his family? He had seemed startled, so maybe not... if he wasn't, this sure was a shitty way to come out to them.

Stalling in the bedroom forever wasn't an option, sadly, so I slowly opened the door to head back out.

The dog had settled down on the floor in front of the sofa, while Caesar and his mother were in the open-plan kitchen.

"Matty." Caesar caught sight of me and hurried over, his hand settling on the small of my back, pushing me forward. "This is my mum. Mum, this is Matt."

"Hello," she greeted me. I swear I saw a smile on her lips and humour in her eyes. Was she *amused*?

"Hi." I scratched awkwardly at the back of my neck, twining some of my hair around my finger. "Nice to meet you." I didn't exactly have an opinion, nice or not, yet, but it was the polite thing to say.

"You too." She opened the bag she'd brought with her and put sandwiches onto a plate. "I bet you're both hungry." *Definitely* humour in her eyes.

"Mum." Caesar's eyes narrowed.

"Don't worry." She laughed. She had the same melodious, infectious laugh as her son, and my eyes were instantly drawn to him. "I'm going to leave these here, then be on my way."

"You just arrived—"

"Yes, but I didn't know you already had company, love." She swept around to kiss his cheek. "Enjoy your breakfast. I'll ring you later." She looked to me next. "It was nice to meet you, Matt. I hope we'll meet again."

"Yeah," I answered lamely, not knowing what else to say.

Once the door clicked shut after her, I caught sight of the dog, still lying on the rug. "Isn't she going to take the dog with her?"

"She's mine." Caesar turned to cast the dog an affectionate glance. "Mum and Dad had her last night since I was going out. I don't like to leave her alone all night."

"You usually stay out all night?" I raised my eyebrows in question.

He shrugged. "It's been known to happen." He turned back to the counter. "How about breakfast then? Or lunch, rather, I suppose. This looks proper good, it does." He grabbed another plate, put one of the sandwiches on it and thrust it at me.

I took a bite, and only as I swallowed did I realise exactly how hungry I was. I hadn't eaten since dinner the day before, and last night had been quite… active and adventurous. This morning too.

"What do you want to do today?" He asked, eating the first sandwich quickly.

"Don't know." I wasn't good at being sociable with people. Never had been.

"What do you normally do when you're not at university?"

I shrugged awkwardly. "I don't really go out

much. I stay at home, read books, listen to music…"

Depressed to the point of self-harm. A right loser, I was.

"We can just stay in, if that's what you want. It's not like we *have* to go out." He grinned disarmingly as he devoured the second sandwich a bit slower than the first one. "I'm all for a day spent on the sofa. Maybe we can go out to a club tonight? It *is* Saturday, after all."

I nodded quickly. "Sounds like a plan."

He leaned in close, grin widening. "Maybe we can have another shag before then too."

Now that had my interest. "I might just have another in me, yeah."

CHAPTER 5

I suggested we go to the only club I knew about—and it was a *gay* club at that. Only reason I *did* know about it, was because my mate Adam worked the bar there.

"I love this club," Caesar professed once we entered. The music was loud, the club was packed, and it was a bit disorienting, to be truthful.

"You come here often?" I had to lean in to shout it in his ear, or he wouldn't hear me over the bass of the obnoxiously loud music. This wasn't my kind of scene at all. How could Adam even work in this?

Speaking of which… my gaze searched for the bar, and true enough, there was Adam. He was in a thigh sleeveless top, which left his muscular and tattooed arms bare to ogle. Not that I could see them clearly from this far away, but still. His blond hair was spiked up, ears pierced, he was tall, fit, *gorgeous*. And sadly taken.

"Want to go say hi to your mate?"

His words startled me, like I'd been caught with my pants down, but then I remembered I told him Adam worked here on our way over. "Y-yeah." If he heard the shake in my voice, he didn't let on, just grinned and led the way through the throng of people.

We positioned ourselves at the bar, both of us leaning our elbows on the counter.

"I'll buy you a drink." Caesar leaned in close to say that, and he nipped my earlobe at the same time.

"Trying to get another shag out of me?" I ran my finger down his stomach teasingly, remembering fondly just what we'd been up to only a couple of hours before.

"Wouldn't complain if that were the outcome." He pulled a tenner out of his pocket and held it ready for when we'd be served.

I bit down on my lower lip, butterflies fluttering about in my stomach all of a sudden. We'd shagged four times now, two last night and two today. If he still wanted to do it, it meant he wasn't getting tired of me. It meant I wasn't shit in bed. Both of which were good and quite the ego-booster. Because Caesar was definitely easy on the eyes—and him I could actually look my fill at without it bothering him. He'd take it as an invitation.

"Hey, mate!" Adam was in front of us, smiling widely at me.

"Hey." I had problems deciding who to look at. I'd had a crush on Adam for... what, *ages* now. And yet here was Caesar, fit, handsome and definitely interested in *me*. I didn't know which one was better-looking, to be honest. I felt a bit inferior next to both of them. If anything, they were the ones who would've looked real good together.

"What can I get you?" He was completely ignoring Caesar, but when my eyes veered to him in question, Adam seemed to realise we were there together. "Oh, hey, friend of Matt's?"

"Yeah." Caesar shook Adam's outstretched hand, smiling politely. "He said this was the best place to go. And I got to admit, it *is* one of my favourite clubs."

"Matt's not big on going out to clubs." Adam shot a teasing grin my way. "How'd you manage to drag him out with you?"

"I only had to ask." It was Caesar's turn to grin teasingly at me, and I rolled my eyes at them both.

"Once this place closes, there's an after party at my flat. Both of you should come!"

I turned back to him, curious. "Nick allows that?" His boyfriend wasn't exactly known for being a party-goer. He was kind of like me—liked to be by himself. Or with Adam, seeing as they lived together.

"Well, he's out of town, isn't he?" I swear Adam's eyes were sparkling at that. "Now, come on, what can I get you lads?"

Caesar rattled off some drink I'd never heard about and Adam set to work mixing it up.

"Seems like an okay bloke, your mate," Caesar yelled into my ear, nipping at my lobe again. He should stop doing that, unless he wanted me to sprout a hard-on in the middle of the club and all the gyrating, half-naked bodies just looking for someone willing to shag.

"He is. He's great." And not just because I was half-way in love with him. He'd been there after my dad died. We hadn't known each other before then, but after the funeral… he'd told me he'd lost his own parents in the very same way I had lost dad. Car accident. A shitty way to lose someone you love. We'd had a connection ever since.

Sadly, he'd been in his current relationship back then too, so I'd never had a chance on him. Also, even more sadly, he only saw me as a friend.

Maybe not so sad anymore.

I glanced at Caesar again, who was taking in the

rest of the club, a half-smile tilting the corner of his lip up. Here was an interesting bloke, who liked me, whom I felt great with, whom I had awesome sex with. He made my life seem brighter from that very moment he'd offered me a drink out of his bottle. He was radiant, he was alive, and he made everything else shine around him.

"Here you go, mate!" Adam set two glasses on the counter and took the money Caesar handed him, counting out the change to hand back. "If you wait here until I'm done cleaning the bar later, we can head back to the flat together."

I nodded at that and Adam wandered off to tend to the other people flocked around the bar. We left him to it, taking our glasses and moving around the club.

"You like to dance?"

"No, not really." I stared at the people out on the dance floor, how they moved, how they rubbed up together like they didn't have a care in the world. It wasn't exactly my kind of thing.

I could very well rub up against Caesar in private, but dancing along to music… no, definitely not something I'd be good at. My sister was the dancer in the family, not me.

Caesar took a long swallow of his drink. I

watched his Adam's apple bob as his throat worked, fascinated by it. "How about a shag?"

"What? Here?" He must be taking the piss.

"Yeah. Well, not here *here*." He motioned around him. "But there's toilets over there. With stalls."

"Oh." I'd never had sex in a public place before, stalls or no stalls. But I'd turned into a right slag since last night when it came to him, so what else could I say? "Lead the way." I was already getting excited, and my skinny jeans weren't the best place to conceal a hard dick. But then again, it'd be free in a matter of minutes, ready for another orgasm.

Bloody hell. I really am turning into a slag.

But how could I possibly complain?

CHAPTER 6

My back rested against the wall, my jeans were flung over the top of the door, and my legs were wrapped firmly around Caesar's waist.

I hadn't realised he'd come prepared for just this, but he *had*. The minute we'd locked ourselves in the stall, he'd brandished a lubed condom. And now he was fucking me nice and slow.

"I thought toilet sex was supposed to be hard and rough?" I nipped on his lower lip, arms locked tight around his shoulders.

"I like to be contradictory." He nipped back on my upper lip. "We'll get to the hard and rough part, eventually." His hands cupped my arse, squeezed, then he grabbed me up close as he turned us around.

He sat down on the toilet so I was now straddling his lap. I moved without being prompted, up and down his length, taking it all the way in before rising up again. I moaned softly, and so did he. It was the most wonderful sound in the *world*. And I might be a bit drunk, considering we'd started drinking at home, and I'd been well on my way to drunk already then.

"Yeah, just like that." Caesar's gaze was locked on my cock, which was hard and bobbing in-between us. Pre-come leaked from the slit, even if neither of us were touching it.

I wonder if I can come like this, from him fucking my arse, without my cock being touched once? I'd seen some people manage it, but then porn wasn't exactly reliable material for proper research into the matter.

"We could've stayed back in your flat for this." Though it was a bit exhilarating to know that whoever came into the toilets could hear us. See us too if they looked under the door or over the stalls, but I didn't think people would be *that* desperate to see two blokes shagging. Though then again...

"Got to get out and live life, right?" He gripped my arse cheeks tighter, helping me move up and down his cock quicker than I'd been doing it on my own. I wasn't used to this kind of activity, this kind of position, so my thighs were already starting to protest.

"By living life you mean—" A loud moan escaped me as he nailed that sweet spot inside, "—shagging in a public toilet?"

"No better way to live it. You really want to live life, you got to shag everywhere you can."

I dropped my head onto his shoulder as I chuckled.

"You don't agree?" He tilted his head to the side, lips brushing over my cheek.

"I do." I did now. Wouldn't have before. He drew something out in me. A sex-mad slag who didn't mind one bit the voyeurism of shagging in a toilet. If anyone had told me last week that my weekend would end up like this, I would've given them my unimpressed death-glare. I was turning into my sister, someone who loved to party and shag blokes —and *eww*, definitely wrong thought to have when *I* was being shagged by a bloke.

Caesar grabbed me tight again and flipped us over, so now my arse was resting against the toilet lid and he was in-between my legs, hips gaining the speed I hadn't been able to while seated on top of him.

"Oh God!" I fumbled behind me to grip the back of the toilet, but this wasn't one of the older types.

This one was built into the wall and all I managed to do was press in the button to flush it.

It startled me so much I almost toppled to the floor, but managed to keep my balance by holding onto the lid itself with white knuckles.

"Priceless, Matty. Priceless." He laughed at me, the sod.

I started to glare, but then he increased his speed further, and everything but the pleasure fled from my mind. I was getting loud again, like I'd discovered I could be last night and it felt too good to even bother with the fact that *everyone* would hear us if they came inside.

Speaking of which, I heard the door open.

He, however, nailed my spot, and any shyness I would've normally felt—or at least I suppose I would've felt—was absent. All that mattered was that he kept fucking me, kept hitting that spot—

Someone rapped on the door. "Got off early. Time for you two to *get off* so we can start drinking." It was Adam—and his voice was full of laughter.

"Fuck off!" I didn't want my mate, especially not the one I had a massive crush on, to listen to me shag another bloke. Or another bloke shag me, whatever.

It only made him laugh louder. "Come on then. I'll go get started on the drinking, and you better hurry up."

Caesar chuckled, deep in his throat, and I stared up at him. His hands were on the back of my thighs, bending my feet up so he had full access *down there*.

"What?" It definitely wasn't funny.

"I think I like him. He's the type of bloke who's not ashamed of sex. Sex is great. It's something to be enjoyed at every opportunity."

"I don't think Adam—" But his sudden hard thrust shut me up, choking me on a groan.

He didn't relent, kept on with the hard, deep thrusting until I came with a shout, semen shooting to the floor, but also on my jumper. It didn't matter at the moment—all that mattered was the pleasure, of milking it out of me, of milking it out of *him*.

And he did come too, with loud groans escaping him as he did so. Once he was finished, he held onto the condom as he pulled out, then was careful as he took it off so the semen wouldn't spill. Once I rose, he flushed it down the toilet.

"Is that such a good idea?" I watched it swirl for a moment before being swallowed down the drain. "What if it gets stuck and clogs it up or something?"

"Oh, Matty." He grabbed me around the neck and pulled me in for a deep kiss.

I answered it, the condom already forgotten as I let my tongue tangle with his. He was a fantastic kisser—it almost made my cock stir again. But only almost. After three orgasms, I was pretty sure I was done for the day.

I knew people said blokes my age thought about sex all the time, and walked around with a stiffy all the time, but being fucked three times, orgasms wrenched from me all three times—I couldn't take anymore today. My arse couldn't take anymore either.

Speaking of arse… Caesar's finger ran down my crack, over the muscle. "Sore?"

"Yeah." No use lying about it. He must know that I was, what with having been fucked twice the night before too, and that had been my first time. I was pretty sure my arse would need *days* to recover from the vigorous fucking it had received in the last twenty-four hours.

When he let me go to do up his trousers, I grabbed my jeans and boxers. I slid on the underwear, then pulled on my jeans, having to jump a bit up and down to get them over my thighs. They were the true definition of skinny jeans, after all.

"Your arse looks so good in those." Caesar pressed up behind me, lips against my neck. "All of you is to die for, but the way these jeans show off your arse—I want to shag you again."

Flattery would get him everywhere, except I

suspected he was laying it on a bit thick. Still, it was nice to hear.

"Let's go have a drink with Adam, then head over to his flat. Flat parties are funnier than clubs." In my opinion, anyway, but then I was a loner. Crowded clubs did nothing for me.

∼

"FINE BLOKE you got yourself there. Proper fit."

Adam leaned in, whispering conspiratorially as Caesar headed off to the toilet. There were a lot of other people gathered in the flat, mates of Adam, but none of them were paying us any attention at the moment.

"Yeah, he is." There was no denying that. Though Adam was just as fine and fit, too. But also off-limits, so there was that.

"I've never heard you mention him before. Where'd you meet?" He bumped my shoulder, excited for details.

"Met last night. Mathilda dragged me out to some party her friends were having. Guess she was tired of me being cooped up in my room. And there he was, offering me a drink where I was sitting all by myself." Like a knight in shining armour—except the armour he'd worn was a vest that showed off his tattoos and flat chest, and instead of a sword he'd come with alcohol.

"Only last night? And you've had sex?" He stared at me, incredible now. "And here I was, thinking you were a bit of a prude."

"A prude?" I snorted. "What's that supposed to mean?"

"That you don't enjoy partying and jumping into bed with people. Or so I thought, anyway." He grinned, chuckling in a low voice. "Must be special this one, then? Considering you just shagged him in a toilet, and I'm guessing you did a lot more shagging before that."

"You'd be right in that guess." I took a sip of my drink, all the while thinking to myself I must be drunk to be sharing such intimate details. I should stop drinking—or shut up. Easier decided than done. The more alcohol I consumed, the more I *wanted* to consume.

Adam bumped my shoulder again, laughing out loud now. "Is it more though, or just sex?"

"Don't know." That had me chewing on my bottom lip. "I wouldn't *mind* if it turned into more." I wouldn't mind at all. For the first time since my dad died, and everything went to hell, I was enjoying myself, enjoying life.

And all of that was because of Caesar.

He hadn't turned me away when he'd seen my scars. They hadn't bothered him last night, and not so much today either, except he'd seemed troubled when he'd asked about them.

"Here he comes." Adam bumped me again, almost sending me sprawling as I was still deep in thought and unprepared for it. He stood to give Caesar his place. "Here you go, mate. We were just having a little chat."

Caesar smiled at me. "What were you chatting about? Or is it a secret?"

I watched Adam walk off to talk to someone else. "Talking about you, actually." I tilted my head to the side, glancing at him. I felt a bit shy, though why I did was beyond me. We'd been the most intimate two people could be—several times. I shouldn't become shy now. "Adam gives his approval."

"Of me?" Caesar splayed his hand over his chest.

"Of course, *you*." I leaned sideways so our shoulders and upper arms pressed together. "He thinks you're right fit."

Caesar turned his head, looking at me from under thick, black lashes. "And do you think I'm right fit?"

There came the shyness again, this time accompanied by a *blush*. "Yeah. I do, actually."

He kissed me, but it was only a lip-on-lip chaste kiss, not like the passionate ones with tongue he'd given me before. "I think you're proper fit too, Matty."

That nickname… He was using it again. Everyone always called me Matt, a shortening for Matthew, but no one had ever given me a—I suppose it could be called a *pet name?*—before. It was sweet, endearing, I liked it. *A lot.*

"Want to leave this place?" I had a sudden urge to have him on my own. It was nice having seen Adam, but I didn't know any of his mates, and the only interest I had right now was to be alone with Caesar.

"I thought you were too sore for more of that," he teased, tilting his head to rest against my temple.

"We don't have to fuck. There's loads of other things we can do." Cuddling, kissing… My hand, of its own volition, moved to cup his crotch and my mouth practically watered at the thought of sucking his cock again. Shagging was amazing, but I was well and truly shagged-out. That didn't mean there weren't other sexual things we could do, though.

Caesar was on his feet before I could do much more than squeeze. "Yeah, you're right, let's go." He took my hand and pulled me to my feet, grinning when I stumbled into him. He pecked my cheek before he turned to drag me towards the door.

"See you, Adam!" I called out.

"Have fun!" I could hear him laughing at my

expense, but it didn't matter. Surely he'd been like this too when he'd just got with Nick—horny *all the time*. Excited about the new prospects.

Adam and Nick had ended up in a relationship. They were on their, what, third or fourth year now? I hadn't known Adam back when they'd got together, but I knew they'd never been casual.

Were Caesar and I casual? Could we move past that to more? Would he even want to, or was sex enough for him? I liked the sex, I *loved* the sex, and it wouldn't be a chore continuing it, no matter what.

"Don't look so sullen." He threw an arm around my neck, drawing me in close to his side. "You should smile more, Matty. Smiling suits you. Think about how much fun we're going to have when we get back to my flat, how good we'll pleasure each other. How much we'll come. I bet you've got a lot more in here." It was his turn to cup my crotch.

A startled chuckle left me.

"There you go." He pecked my cheek. "Smiling."

For him I could smile. Because he made me forget what my life was like otherwise. When I was with him, I felt loose and happy, and that... was something I hadn't felt in so long.

CHAPTER 7

"*W*here the hell have you been?"

Mathilda materialised in front of me the minute I entered the flat. Her hair was loose, hanging down her back and over her shoulder, and she had her hands firmly planted on her hips. Her expression was stormy.

"Out." I tried to slip past her, but she only moved to block my way.

"We've been worried *sick* about you! I tried texting you, ringing you—but you never answered!"

"My phone's dead." It had died sometime on Friday, so I hadn't even bothered bringing it out with me.

"*You* could've been dead!" Her hands left her hips and instead connected with my chest, startling me so much I stumbled back into the wall. "*Dead*, you hear me? Fucking *dead*!" She hit my chest for emphasis.

"Mathilda!" Josh came around the corner, out of the kitchen, and behind him came Damian.

"Don't *Mathilda* me!" She was at the point of crying. "He's been gone the whole weekend. He doesn't even bother to ring home and tell us he's fine."

"I'm sorry," I murmured. It hadn't even occurred to me. I'd been enjoying myself too much to even spare a thought for how they must've felt. "Besides, it's not like you're one to talk." I shouldn't jibe her, but I couldn't help it. It was only a couple years since *she'd* been the one out partying all the time, staying out at all hours.

"Don't be smart with me!" Her fist hit my chest again. "You were here—you should've *learned* from my mistakes, shouldn't you?"

Well, yes. I'd seen how worried Mum had been back then. How worried Damian and Josh had been, too. I'd told myself I'd never make them worry like that, and now I had.

Guilt gnawed at me from the inside, and I slowly lifted my head to look at them. Damian was expressionless, but Josh was easier to read where he twisted his hands nervously, glancing from me to Mathilda and back again.

"I'm sorry, I was—" too busy being shagged. "I was with a mate."

"You've been with Adam?" Mathilda stepped back, on a safe distance where hopefully her fists wouldn't be hitting me again anytime soon.

"No. Someone else."

"Adam's your only mate." Her eyes narrowed suspiciously. "Alistair said he saw you leave with Caesar. You've been with him all weekend? *Caesar*, of *all* people?"

She said his name like he wasn't even worthy of being the dirt on her shoes and it riled me. It riled me up proper. "What the hell is that supposed to mean? That tone of yours?"

"I haven't got a *tone*. I've got an opinion, and that opinion is that Caesar isn't a good person to be around."

"How can you stand here and say something like that? Do you *know* him?" I knew she didn't. Caesar had already said he didn't know her.

"I know *of* him, and that's more than enough." She crossed her arms over her chest, defensive.

"Well, *I* know him!" Not really, but for the sake of the argument... "And he happens to be a very nice person."

"Of course he acts like that. To get what he wants." She was so bloody stubborn. I didn't know who she'd got that from, neither Mum nor Dad was ever like that.

"And what is it he wants?" My tone turned dangerously low.

"A shag, obviously! He's known for that, you know, that he shags *everyone*!"

"Do I have to remind you who else here was known as quite the slag?" That hit home. She took a step back, like she'd been stricken, her lips parting in a low gasp. "Would you've liked it if someone went warning people off of you? Because I'm sure they did, Mathilda. Back in college, they liked to talk about you. How easy it was to get you on your back!"

I had never wanted to divulge that information. Hearing someone say such things about my sister had been too much to handle, and I'd never wanted her to hear it either.

She'd taken it really badly after Dad had died and she'd done things I suppose she wasn't so proud of now... but the truth of the matter was that it *was* truth. She'd been sleeping around. So she had no business slandering on Caesar.

I couldn't stand there and face her anymore though, so I brushed past them—Josh and Damian were still there—to head for my room.

"Well, I'm not the only one on my back anymore,

am I?" she yelled after me, having got over the initial shock, apparently.

I stopped in front of my door, slowly turning around so I could see her.

She was furious.

Damian was slightly turned away, fingers pressed against his temple.

Josh glanced between us, uncertain and nervous.

"At least I'm on my back for one person. I don't go messing about with a whole lot of them." With that delivered, I entered my room and slammed the door shut. I even locked it for effect.

I fell face down on my bed, trembling with anger. She had a way of worming under my skin until I got *so* angry I combusted. It was her superpower—to annoy and anger me. She could get me raging in seconds, exactly like she had with her jab about Caesar. She should be the bloody *last* person to slander someone else. *The last!*

Once I calmed, I flipped over onto my back, staring up at the ceiling.

I confirmed we've shagged.

I just came out to them.

I hadn't said the word *gay*, but I didn't have to. Admitting to shagging another bloke told loud and clear where my interest lay.

Oh God. Oh God. I shouldn't be freaking out.

Damian and Josh were gay and in a relationship, for God's sake. They had been together for what, six years now, ever since I was a pre-pubescent little brat. I didn't have a problem with them, and I knew they wouldn't have a problem with me, and it wasn't like I was ashamed of what I'd done this weekend… yet why couldn't I admit to people what I was? That I liked blokes, that I loved cock, that I liked being fucked.

The latter two would be too much information, but the first one… It shouldn't be a hard thing to say. But it was a thing that had *always* been hard. It was something I'd never managed to tell my own parents —and now I couldn't tell Dad anymore, because he'd been dead for over three years. And Mum… she'd fucked off with her new bloke. I'd never once even so much as hinted at being gay.

I sat up to rummage through my bedside drawer, where I drew out a small book and a pencil. I sat cross-legged and opened the journal up to the last page I'd written on.

Josh was the one in the family who was big with words. He'd started with journals, then gone on to blogging and writing books. Me, on the other hand, could only seem to write in *poetry*. Shitty poetry at that. I wasn't anywhere close to being the next Shakespeare or anything like it.

But it did serve a therapeutic purpose, I suppose. I wasn't seeing a therapist, no matter how much Damian and Josh had been on me about that after Dad died.

What did I need a bloody therapist for? So they could prop me full of pills? *I think not.*

But writing my words down, even if it was just in poetry form, helped a lot.

I ran my finger over the left page, where I'd last written on Friday, a few hours before Mathilda had forced me out of bed to go to that party with her.

> *Behind a scar, a story, they say*
> *A tale of pain, of grief, of trauma*
> *Never escaping the feelings within*
> *Consuming me, dragging me down,*
>   *burying me*
> *The relief, a blade, slicing*
> *The sight of blood, calming*
> *After comes shame, hate*
> *No matter, as long as skin is pierced*

I hadn't actually cut myself on Friday, though I likely would have if Mathilda hadn't been so bloody persistent. I was grateful for that now, for how she wouldn't take no for an answer. How she'd ripped my duvet off the bed to get a reaction out of me. For how she'd shoved me into the bathroom to take a shower and get ready.

If it hadn't been for her, I wouldn't have met Caesar. And no matter what Mathilda said about him, he was *good*. He was good for me.

I'd found someone I was interested in who showed an interest back, and she should be happy for me instead of condemning him.

Wasn't it good that I was happy for once? That I was out instead of being cooped up in my room, as was the norm whenever I wasn't at uni? She had to get over herself. What did it matter to her anyway who I was mates with? Who I did *more* than be friends with?

Something moved out of the corner of my eye, and I chanced a quick glance that way. Nothing. Only shadows. *That's what I get for painting my room in a dark colour, I guess. And for having an overactive imagination.*

I focused back on my notebook, running my finger over the right page, the empty one. I had to write something, the words were slowly forming in my head. I grabbed the pencil and put it to paper, the entire poem coming effortlessly.

This feeling
happy, excited

> *To see him, to feel him*
> *to be around him*
> *A deep sleep*
> *like a veil over my eyes*
> *Lifted, disappeared*
> *Replaced by*
> *him, live and breathing*
> *Loving life*
> *bringing light*
> *into mine*

It was a good thing I wasn't doing this for a living. It was only a recreational hobby, a hobby that sometimes kept me from my razor blade. And sometimes both pencil and blade had to be in use to stop the heavy thoughts.

Speaking of which…

The blade was in the drawer as well and I lifted it out reverently. I hadn't cut since Thursday. Usually I had a hard time going so long between, but with Caesar everything had seemed so much *lighter*.

Caesar was back at his flat now, snuggled up on his sofa with his dog. At least he had been when I'd left and I didn't see a reason for him to have changed that. Unless he was out finding someone else to shag. But no… I didn't think he'd be doing that either.

He had work in the morning, and I… I had

nothing to go to. I had the whole summer holiday stretching endlessly out in front of me. Nothing to look forward to, nothing to do but stay in my room.

My room was my sanctuary. It was the place that knew all my secrets, the place that saw all the darkness, but it was also my sanctuary. In here I was safe, no matter how depressed I was, no matter how little I wanted to deal with the world. This was *my* place and no one came in here unless given permission.

Damian and Josh were big on privacy, I'd give them that. They didn't nag, like Mum had a tendency to do, back before when I lived with her. Before Dad had died. *Clean your room, pick up your clothes, make your bed.*

Though, I did all those things anyway now, because they'd been there for me, they'd let me move in when I couldn't stand to be around Mum anymore.

They were only in their mid-twenties, not yet settled in their own lives, and yet they'd taken care of me. Mum had sold our house after Dad died, and I still resented her for that. We hadn't got along. So I got to live with Josh and Damian. They'd found a flat on their own, with more than one bedroom, where I could live with them.

I often wondered what I'd have done if they hadn't been there, if they hadn't taken me in. I didn't have any kind of income. Maybe I could've got into the dorms after I started university, but what about before I finished college?

Don't think about that. It served no purpose. It was a what-if situation that hadn't happened. They had taken me in, I had a place to live, a place to call home.

And I was grateful to them for doing that. For sacrificing their, presumably, comfortable life—they had shared a flat with two mates, another couple, previously. They'd seemed happy with that arrangement.

Grateful… And yet I was being a twat. Staying away for two nights without a word to them. Mathilda was right; I could've been dead for all they knew.

A shitty thing to do, Matt. Real shitty.

I rolled up my left sleeve to look at my skin. There were a lot of scars criss-crossing each other. Some deeper than others. The most recent cuts, from Thursday, weren't that deep and they'd probably heal without leaving much evidence of having been there at all. But still, I had so many others that wouldn't ever go away.

How could Caesar have seen this on Friday night and just ignored it? Was he that desperate for a shag? Didn't it matter what I looked like, as long as sex happened?

Or maybe he didn't think you were ugly at all, even when the scars were revealed.

I didn't know where that voice came from. Spouting bullocks. How could the scars *not* be ugly?

My right hand shook, twitching closer to my left one. I had to do it. *Have to.* I couldn't keep going back and forth in my mind, ridden by guilt one minute and beating myself down the next. I'd go mental if I continued like that.

So I cut myself.

CHAPTER 8

A cut
a wound
a scar
Skin's a mess
A blade,
causing harm
A craving
a yearning
an addiction
Can't stop,
unless harm
is done

I shuffled into the living room, where I found Damian and Josh curled up on the sofa. Or, Josh was curled up against Damian, head on his shoulder and eyes closed. Damian was sitting facing the telly, legs spread wide, one arm around Josh, fingers playing with his hair.

It was so simple, yet so intimate.

Jealous. That's how I felt. I wanted that with someone. To just curl up. I wanted the simple things. Sex was great, of course, I wouldn't be without it now I'd learned how amazing it could be, but this... this was a proper relationship. This was love.

"Hey." I took the other sofa, curling up myself, a bit like Josh. The sleeves of my jumper were bunched up in my palms, mostly to make sure they wouldn't slip up reveal what I'd just been doing to myself. There was a burning sort of pain going up my forearm, the *good* sort.

"Hey." Damian regarded me, face still void of any expression. That was normal for him though, he was impossible to read. Only Josh managed to, and that was because they'd been together for so long.

Josh opened his eyes, and he blinked at me. He, too, was wearing long sleeves, so I couldn't see the skin on his arms. I knew his were a lot worse than mine. He had scars all over, not just his forearms, but his upper arms and shoulders as well. As far as I'd seen when Josh wore short sleeves, there wasn't a single piece of unscarred skin on either of his arms.

I wondered, if I didn't get myself sorted out, if I would end up exactly like him. It was already pretty bad.

"I'm sorry. I really am." I glanced between them, hoping they'd see I was sincere. "I should've texted or rang you, but I just... I forgot. I'm really, really sorry." The guilt ate me up.

"It's okay, Matt." Josh straightened up a bit. "Just remember to do it next time, okay?"

They were too kind. Mum and Dad would've both pitched a fit if I'd done this to them, back then. They might've not grounded me, me being eighteen now and all now, but they sure wouldn't be happy with me—and they'd show it. As long as I lived at home, I had to live by their rules. That's what they'd told both me and Mathilda countless times over the years.

After Dad died, Mum had changed too. It was like we'd lost both our parents that day. Mum had been depressed, not really cared what we did anymore. And then she'd met that new bloke.

"I will." I'd keep that promise too. They were the only family I had—well, they, Mum, and my aunt, but she didn't live in London anymore. I loved them,

I *did*, and I never wanted them to worry about me. I worried enough myself, about everything. I couldn't let on how messed up I really was. They had enough to deal with just having me under their roof, when that hadn't been in their life-plan at all.

I bit my lip, pondering what to say. I had to say *something*. "I appreciate everything you've done for me."

Both their gazes, which had veered back to the telly during my silence, snapped back to me. "What'd you mean?"

"Taking me in, dealing with everything." *Dealing with Mum.* "I know I haven't been easy." I'd been easy in the sense that I'd hardly left my room, but perhaps that was cause for more concern from them than if I had gone out.

Mathilda had hardly been home in the beginning after Dad died. Mum had been too grief-stricken to notice or care. But Josh and Damian had... I wasn't sure what was most worrisome though. Staying cooped up in my bedroom, or Mathilda off shagging every bloke she could find.

The grief had been all-consuming. I hadn't been able to face the world. I remembered Josh bringing me breakfast every day for... a great many days after the funeral. I'd never touched it. I hadn't even been able to face *food*.

"Of course we took you in. What else could we have done? " Josh rearranged himself so he was sitting cross-legged. Damian's arm rested along the back on the sofa now, instead of around his shoulders. "I don't know why you and your Mum fell out exactly, because as far as we know, you don't ever *do* anything. You just stay in your room. But you'll always have a home with us, Matt."

Damian nodded in agreement to Josh's words, gazing briefly at him before turning his attention back to me.

His gaze was intense and I dropped my head to stare at my hands. Or the sleeves of my jumper, considering my hands were bunched up inside.

"I'm glad you've had an enjoyable weekend."

My head snapped up, just as Josh seemed to realise his choice of verb wasn't the best, considering what had been revealed about my weekend activities in my shouting match with Mathilda.

"That was—well…" He scratched at his cheek and neck, eyes going to Damian who was carefully looking the other way. "I'm glad you had a nice *time* this weekend." He didn't seem to be happy with that choice of words either, but he settled for it.

"Caesar's really great," was all that came out of me. I must have developed a crush already, speaking without filtering myself.

"Is he your age?" Josh seemed to be genuinely interested, which warmed me.

"Yeah. Well, two years older, but that's not much." We were the same age-group, anyway. "Is Mathilda here?" I bit my lip again, nervous now. "I should apologise to her."

"Yeah. You should." Josh nodded, a bit stern, a bit sympathetic. "You said some cruel things to her. But she should apologise too. You were both in the wrong.."

"She's in her room." This was Damian, finally weighing in, jerking his head towards said door.

I pursed my lips, then jumped off the sofa to get it over with. Mathilda was usually easy-going, though stubborn and able to hold a grudge if something didn't go her way. And I'd definitely been a little harsh towards her earlier.

"Mathilda?" I knocked tentatively on her door. No answer. "Mathilda? Please."

I heard a muffled *come in*, so I pressed the door handle down and slipped into her room as soon as the gap was big enough. I closed the door softly after me.

Her room was nothing like mine. My room was *mine*, whereas Mathilda was only occupying Josh and Damian's guest room. The walls weren't covered in posters, nor was it full of all her things. She only had a suitcase open at the foot of her bed, and random stuff strewn around that would be easy to dump back into the suitcase again once Mum came home.

Mathilda was at the desk, laptop on and Facebook open in a tab. She swivelled around on her chair to face me, and her expression was the epitome of someone not about to take any more shit. "What do you want?"

"I'm sorry." I scuffed my toes against the fluffy rug. "For what I said. I was angry and it just came out, but that's no excuse. So… I'm really sorry."

She swivelled back around to face her laptop.

"Mathilda…" Was she really going to do this? I was *apologising*.

"You were right, you know."

I blinked. "What?"

"About what you said. About me. You were right. I just… I didn't know you knew about the rumours, considering you never really talked to anyone." Her head was bent now, her long hair shielding her face from view even if I leaned over.

"Just because I never talked to anyone, doesn't mean they didn't talk to each other in my presence." I wasn't sure people knew I even was present, but still… I'd heard the rumours. "But rumours… they're usually lies, or at least the truth blown out of proportion."

"It wasn't." She turned back around quickly, facing me with a set expression. "It wasn't blown out of proportion. It was true." She drew her lower lip into her mouth, chewing on it. "Everything felt so... I don't know, wrong? And I just... It got a bit wild. But I've changed since then. I'm not—not like that anymore."

I nodded, feeling extremely uncomfortable having my sister chatting about her sex life. It was even worse hearing it from her, than to hear someone else gossip about it. Or at least it was on equal ground.

"I'm sorry for what I said about Caesar. Out of everyone, I know I shouldn't go around taking rumours to heart. Maybe he's changed too."

Well, I didn't know about that, considering I'd never even heard of him before Friday night. "He's great."

"I think it's awesome that you've met someone. I really do." I could tell she was sincere by the way her eyes were a bit wider than normal, like she was begging me to believe in her.

"Thanks." I scuffed my toe against the fluffy rug again.

"So... you're gay, huh? You never said." Her chair creaked as she moved.

"No." I still couldn't believe I'd actually come out to her—to *them*. And the *way* I'd done it.

"How long have you known for?"

"Years, I guess."

She blinked at that, startled. "Why'd you never tell?"

I shrugged. "Don't know." It was a very good question I kept asking myself. I never had a proper, well-thought out answer for it.

"I don't mind, you know. Not at all."

"I know." I knew none of them would mind. Maybe I suffered from internalised homophobia.

Then again, maybe not. I wasn't the least bit ashamed of the weekend's happenings. And considering I'd shagged Caesar in a public toilet, with *Adam* listening in, that said something.

Maybe I was just a coward, then, unable to tell people who I really was. Like with the cutting…

My arm flashed in pain, like it had read my mind and wanted to remind me what I'd just done to it.

"Chat with you later, okay?" A sudden need to be alone rose in me, bubbling up, almost choking me. I escaped from her room before she could say anything else, hurrying past Damian and Josh, and into my own room where I swiftly closed the door after me.

I leant against the sturdy door, taking in my private

space, my sanctuary. It was painted a dark blue, but posters lined most of the walls. Posters of rock and metal bands. A bookcase to my side, crammed full of course books and fantasy fiction books and comics. A desk across, with my laptop, a mountain of notebooks and pencils and pens scattered all over. And then my bed, to my left, up against the wall.

The sheets, black, because everything in my life was black, were bunched after I'd been sitting there earlier. The razor blade was back in my bedside table drawer, along with the cloth I'd used to dry up the blood. Couldn't leave evidence out in the open, *in case* someone were to come in.

I spotted my mobile on my desk and it brought me into action. It was still dead, so I put it on to charge. I'd given Caesar my number before I'd left his place earlier, and I wanted my phone to be on and ready if he were to text me.

I sure hoped he would.

With that done, I couldn't think of anything else to do, so I lay down on the bed again. I had stars in my ceiling, the kind that glowed in the dark. They were fascinating, though at the moment it was too light for them to glow.

I slowly peeled my left sleeve up to take a look at my arm. Some more blood had trickled, smeared over my skin, but most of the cuts had stopped bleeding already. I hadn't cut that deep—and I'd *never* cut so deep I'd had to have sutures. I'd come close though, as some of the most brutal scars could attest to.

So ugly, yet so fascinating.

I ran my fingers over the scarred skin, liking the feel of it, liking the sight of it. When I was alone, I thought this was art, beautiful. It was only when other people came around I realised it wasn't, that it was *bad*, that I probably *did* need help. Serious help.

I'd never heard Josh speak about his scars as if he *liked* having them there. Because he didn't like them. If he could, he'd be rid of them all.

Sometimes, that was my wish too. But most of the time, especially when I was alone, they felt like they were a special part of me. A part no one else knew about.

The scars, and being gay, had been something only I had known about, something I'd kept close. Now one secret was out of the bag—and I definitely didn't want the other one to be revealed. I didn't think anyone would take that okay.

Except maybe Josh. Who'd found out about my cutting three years ago, before Dad died. But back then it had only been scratches really. It wasn't until after Dad was gone that it escalated into *this*.

I sighed and craned my neck to stare over at my

phone. Nothing going on over there. Silent like the grave.

"Grave." I snorted, eyes falling closed. I let my injured arm rest on my chest, loving the tingling of pain my jumper left as it rubbed against the cuts.

Three years ago I'd been standing in front of an open grave, watching my Dad's coffin being lowered into it. I'd seen it, I'd been right there next to it—but I'd felt so detached.

Mathilda had been crying for days, ever since she found out he was dead, all through the funeral and the next days. And me… I hadn't been able to. I still hadn't cried *once*. Not for Dad.

Last year, when my dog died though… Then I'd lost it. One of the deepest cuts, the biggest scar, had been put on my arm then.

Something's definitely wrong with me.

I couldn't cry for my own Dad, but I had for my dog. I liked the cutting, the scars. Mostly, anyway. I liked being on my own—unless it was Caesar and we were shagging. Or Adam. I wasn't opposed to being around Adam either.

But other than that, my life consisted of my room, books, music and bad poetry. A sad life it was. Or should be anyway. But I preferred it. Being on my own, not living up to other people's expectations, just being *me*.

All I had to keep me company was the razor—and the shadows that seemed to move when I didn't have my eyes on them. When I did look, all was still, but when I didn't… I should've painted my room in a light colour, perhaps, but then again, that didn't fit with my life. The damn shadows were just my imagination going haywire.

Nothing there, nothing there, nothing there!

I craned my neck to look at my phone again. Still silent. *Isn't he going to text? I've been home hours now.* My chest squeezed tight, almost to the point of painful. But my phone stayed silent, all through the evening and through the night.

CHAPTER 9

Caesar: Want 2 meet up after I finish work?

I stared at the screen, then down at my right arm. He'd contacted me, like I'd been wanting him to do ever since we'd parted the day before—but my arm was too much of a mess.

The blood wasn't trickling slowly today, like it had on the left arm yesterday—it was flowing nicely, like a river, coming to an end at my wrist or hands or fingers and slowly dripping into the tub, colouring the white red.

Me: Can't.

It physically hurt me to type that in and send it, even more than the deep cuts I'd inflicted on myself.

He instantly texted a sad-face in return and my stomach twisted in guilt and remorse and hopelessness. If only he'd texted just a bit earlier, before I'd locked myself in the bathroom with my razor blade.

Me: Sorry.

My heart beat steadily against my chest as a thought-cloud appeared, telling me he was writing something back.

Caesar: Do U want 2 see me?

Me: Yeah.

Caesar: Then how come U can't? Other plans?

Me: No. No plans.

Caesar: Matty. Why then?

I swallowed heavily, trying to dislodge the lump that had decided to get stuck in my throat. The thumb of my left hand awkwardly typing up my next text to him.

Me: I cut myself.

Caesar had already seen the scars, and he hadn't minded them. Being honest with him was probably the best way to go. It wasn't like I knew what to lie about, if I hadn't decided on the truth.

It took him longer to answer me this time. My heart beat faster, deathly afraid he'd decided that the shagging wasn't worth these kinds of issues.

Caesar: Bad?

Matt: I guess, yeah.

Caesar: What's yr address? Coming over.

I sat up in a panic at that, then calmed myself down with deep breaths. It wasn't like he was outside the door. He wasn't even done at work yet—which meant it'd be a while until he arrived. I'd have time to clean up.

I typed in my address and sent it to him, panic replaced by relief now that he still wanted to see me. That he'd come over here when I hadn't been able to go out. My reason for not wanting to see him had been my cutting, which would still be an issue if he came around here, but… well, now he knew.

And having him over here, in my room, when no one else was home… it felt a bit naughty, a bit forbidden, like we would be doing something we shouldn't be. Which was weird, because I was over eighteen and legal to do everything we could possibly think of doing.

But thinking of doing it under Damian and Josh's roof… well, it felt weirder than back at Caesar's flat. There we'd had no inhibitions, being as loud as we felt like. Here, on the other hand, I didn't think I could give myself over to the pleasure quite that way, no matter if anyone was home or not.

Caesar: c u in a bit!

That spurred me into motion again. I had to clean my arm, wrap it up, change my clothes, throw the dirty, bloody clothes in the washer before anyone else saw them—and then I should clean my room. *Caesar* was coming over, it had to be spotless!

It was a good thing no one was home, because if they'd been, they'd wonder why I was running around like a madman. I only stopped moving once the doorbell rang, standing rigid in the middle of my bedroom floor.

He's here! It felt like no time had passed at all, but it must've.

I approached the front door with a dash of trepidation, a dash of excitement, and a dash of lust, because really, how could I not feel that considering what we'd spent our weekend doing?

He smiled brilliantly at me as I opened the door, and I smiled back, chest tight from a happiness I wasn't used to feeling. "Come in." I stepped aside and he brushed past me, looking around curiously once he was inside the flat.

"My room's right over here." I led him across the living room and let him walk first into my bedroom, so I could go last and lock the door after me.

Caesar took a good look around, then headed over to my bookcase. He perused what I had in there, then seemed to be drawn to what was tacked on the wall next to it. It was the only place that wasn't filled with posters—instead there were pictures.

I stepped up close to him, pointing to a picture in the middle. "That's my parents." They were smiling into the camera. Dad had his arm around Mum's shoulder and Mum's was around his waist.

"You look a lot like your dad, but I can see some of your mum in you too."

That warmed me. That I looked like my dad, anyway. I knew I looked like my dad, both me and Mathilda did. And Damian. He could've passed for his son too, not just his nephew.

Speaking of which… "There's Damian and Josh. My cousin and his boyfriend. This is their flat." It was a picture of them taken at a barbie at our house some summers ago. They weren't as affectionate in their picture as Mum and Dad were in theirs, but then they never really were when there were other people around.

For all I knew, they weren't even affectionate when they were alone.

"He looks like you too." Caesar pointed at Damian, which I had expected.

"Dad and his mum were twins." I refrained from telling him more about Damian's mum though and what a mental case she'd been—killing her whole family.

It was something I never heard Damian talk about, but Mum and Dad had told us what had happened back when Damian came to live with us, even if we'd been too young at the time to understand exactly how gruesome it had been.

"You and Mathilda are twins, right?" He cast a curious look my way.

"Yeah." I ran my hand over a picture of her next. She was in her dancing gear, practicing some number out on our lawn. An old picture, but still accurate, considering she was now pursuing a university degree in dance. "Runs in the family that, doesn't it?"

"Think I've heard that somewhere, yeah." He touched another picture, this one of Adam and his older brother, who was a mate of Josh and Damian's. It was thanks to them I'd properly got to know Adam. "Your mate from this weekend." He took a step back to survey all the images. They were put in a semi-circle sort of form. "All these people... you know them?"

"Well, yeah. They're family, friends, acquaintances. But yeah, I know them. Not that I spend any personal time with all of them, but they're great." There were pictures of Josh's whole family, of Damian's best mate and his boyfriend, all the people I met on a regularly basis.

"Nice to be surrounded by so many people."

"I'm not, really. I like being on my own, but those pictures... well, it reminds me I'm not alone, not completely. Dad might be gone, but... I've got a lot of other people here for me, if I allow them to be. Many of them are friends of Damian and Josh, but they're all very close and inclusive."

Caesar headed over to perch on the edge of my bed. I pressed play on my ancient CD-player on my way over to join him, just in case things turned heated and someone came home while we were busy.

"My room feels so bare compared to yours." He lay back on his elbows, grinning at me.

"Somehow I can't see you pasting your walls full of rock posters." I sat cross-legged, facing him.

"Why not?"

"Don't know. Just can't." My gaze was running over him, taking note of every single feature. The straight, dark hair, the eyeliner-framed eyes, the big glasses, the pierced lobes, the flat stomach... I wished he wasn't wearing a zipped jumper, because I wanted to see the sinewy muscles in his arms too, as well as his tattoos. I still wasn't quite sure what they were of. I'd been too busy with other things this weekend to take proper notice of them.

He gazed up at me, grey-green eyes bright behind the lenses.

Something stirred in me. More accurately, in my nether regions. "Do you actually need the glasses or are they just for fashion?"

"Both." He grinned. "I see better with glasses, but going without is fine too. I just can't see as well at a distance."

It didn't really matter if he needed them or not. All that mattered was he looked really hot in them. Not to mention his lips, which were slightly parted... begging to be kissed. So I did—I bent down and kissed them.

One of Caesar's hands tangled in my hair. I pushed further down and forward, which undid his precarious balance on only one elbow. He fell back and I followed, our noses smashing together.

"Ow, shit." I chuckled as I rolled over to the side, lying next to him. I felt my nose. Tender, but nothing else. We hadn't hit each other hard enough for much else.

"You're a danger, you." He bumped my side playfully, but he hit my injured arm and as I drew in a sharp breath, he stilled. His head tilted over to look at me. "Why do you cut yourself?"

"Don't know."

"You said on Saturday it was to dull the pain. The emotional pain."

"Well, yeah. Most of the time." I stared up at the ceiling, at my stars. "Sometimes I do it because I *want* to feel something, because I'm numb. Other times I do it because I'm just bored. Because it's fascinating."

"To cut?"

"To see the blood."

"Which one was today?"

"A mix of depression and boredom." Depression because I hadn't heard from him. It was too silly to say, though. If he knew I cut because of him, because I acted like a silly teenager, he certainly wouldn't be impressed with me.

Caesar pushed up on one elbow now, leaning over me. "You aren't doing it for—I mean, because you want to like, die, or something?" His gaze searched my face.

His words startled me. They shouldn't, because cutting your own skin immediately brought to mind suicide, but... "No. I don't want to die."

"Good." He said it with conviction, like it was majorly important to him that I didn't. *Maybe it is.* That had my heart beating double speed in my chest.

He must've seen something, or noticed the change in me, because next I knew his lips were on mine. Soft and skilled, knowing exactly what to do to me. His tongue was no less skilled, drawing moans from me, lighting my body on fire.

I grabbed his waist, pulling him down further so he was lying on top of me, our chests pressed together. He moved a bit, getting his other arm out from under me and instead resting it next to my head.

"Wait—what's this?" He broke the kiss, hand fumbling for something tangled up in the duvet.

I stared as he drew out my journal, then spiralled into movement as I grabbed it from it. "That's nothing."

"Yeah. Obviously." His eyes were laughing at me, I swear. "You write a journal?"

"No." It came out a bit crass. "I mean, not that's there's anything bad about writing a journal, but it's not. It's just… it's poetry."

His eyebrows rose in wonder. "You write poetry?"

"It's not any good, but yeah." I leaned over to deposit the book on the bedside table, then scooted in close to him again. He was watching me, still with eyes that seemed to be laughing. "What is it?"

He shook his head, smiling. "You. You dress all in black, have a lip-piercing, look like the stereotypical emo, you know. And then I find out you're a university student, studying Literature, nonetheless. You're a cutter, but you're not suicidal. You write poetry, but you don't think you're any good. You were eager to have sex, and you *loved* it once we did. Well, at least I *hope* so."

"I did," I whispered. "Greatest thing I ever experienced." I lifted my leg to rest over his calf.

"You're intriguing, Matty." He put his hand on my stomach, the other bracing his head. His fingers pulled my jumper up, then slipped under to find bare skin.

I sucked in a breath at the contact, blood immediately rushing south.

Caesar's chuckle was low, palm pressing further against my skin, sliding up my stomach, over my ribs, over my chest, over my nipples, which puckered right up. Caesar chuckled again, fingers trailing over the hard nubs. "Like that, do you?"

"Yeah." I was breathless already.

He pushed my jumper and tee up, bunching them under my armpits, then bent to suck a nipple into his mouth.

"Oh, *Jesus*!" I managed a strangled moan, fingers going for his head, tangling in his hair.

"Wrong name there, mate." He nipped me teasingly, which only earned him a gasp and an arch of my back up against him in return. He grinned against my skin, then moved over to the opposite nipple, alternating between sucking and nibbling.

"Oh, bloody hell!" My head tilted backwards as I tried to push further up against him. He held me down though, with his weight and his hands, mouth continuing to work on my nipple.

It was too much. I couldn't think clearly, I couldn't see straight… but when he finally let off and instead pulled on my jumper, wanting to get it over my head and off my arms, I let out a strangled shout of pain as it tugged against my injured arm.

"Shit! Matty?"

I curled up on my side. It hurt *so* bad. I fought tears, and I had to win the fight because I sure didn't want to start bawling in front of him.

"I'm sorry." He was sitting next to me but I didn't dare to look up from where my face was buried in the duvet. The tears were still pressing, threatening to fall and make an absolute twat of me. "Matty…"

Several deep breaths later, the pain subsided enough for me to uncurl. I sat up slowly, stared down at my jumper, which was only attached to that arm. I slowly, very carefully, peeled it off.

Caesar sucked in air as he saw the blood-dotted bandage. "That doesn't look so good, Matt. Maybe you should go to A&E. I'll go with you."

"No." I cradled my arm close, but not close enough for anything to press against it and cause further pain. "It's not *that* deep."

"You're still bleeding. I think that proves it's deep."

"It looks worse than it is." I hoped, anyway.

"But—"

"Caesar, please. No A&E." I leaned over, leaning against him. "It hasn't had a chance to start healing yet. I only stopped cutting when you sent your first text."

His arm inched around my shoulder, hesitantly at first, but then settled surely. "If it doesn't stop soon, you'll have to go, Matty. Blood loss is no trivial thing."

"It will stop." It had before. I'd never once had to

go to A&E—I wasn't about to start doing that now. I lifted my head, tilting it up so I could look up at him. "As long as you're careful with my arm, I'd very much like to get back to what we were doing."

His gaze instantly heated at that. "You sure?" Yet he was still hesitating.

Bloody cutting.

"Very sure." I yanked him the few centimetres down until our lips met, kissing him passionately.

We sank down on the bed again, me on my back and him resting on top of me. I knew I had him now —he was vulnerable to sex, and as long as it got him off thoughts of the A&E, I was using it. Not that I minded it, because this was just as pleasurable for me as it was for him.

Maybe we were on an equal footing, maybe it was more for me, I didn't know. All I knew was I'd grown addicted to him in the few days we'd known each other. I craved my next fix and I was getting it now, and that was *all* that mattered.

CHAPTER 10

*K*nock, knock.

I was startled awake so fast I almost rolled out of bed—if it hadn't been for the strong arm around my waist holding me in place on top of the mattress.

"Matt, dinner!" Damian called through the door.

"I have a visitor!" I got out through the panic at being woken so abruptly.

"There's more than enough food." He must've walked away, because he didn't say anything else.

"Hey, *shhh*." Caesar stroked his palm over my chest. My bare chest.

"That knock startled me." Damian tended to knock quickly, in rapid succession. Josh was gentler when he knocked, and so was Mathilda. Unless she was mad at me.

"I can see that." Caesar sat up, his hand falling from my chest. "I can leave if you want."

"Why would I want that?" I stared at him over my shoulder.

"Dinner with your family..." He trailed off as he motioned between the door and me. "You don't actually want me to meet them, do you?"

"I do, actually. Why wouldn't I?"

"Oh." He was the one who seemed startled now. "Okay then."

"Don't you want to meet them?" I wasn't going to force him to stay if he'd rather not.

"I do, I just—" He broke himself off, shaking his head. Then he peered up at me almost sheepishly from underneath his fringe. "No one ever wants me to meet their family."

Something stabbed at my chest. "I want you to." I squeezed his hand, the one that was braced against the bed. "Come on, let's go eat."

Leaving my room would require clothes, though, and I scooped them up from the floor. I threw Caesar's at him and pulled on my own. "You think they can smell it?" I smelled my shirt for emphasis.

"Smell what?"

"You know—sex." Not that it was my shirt that

would smell of sex, it had come off before the sex had happened.

"Don't think so. We just wanked off. It's not like we got all hot and sweaty and jizzed all over."

He had a point. I was too sore for penetrative sex, even if that was what I'd really wanted to do, so we'd just stroked each other—and added some sucking in too. It'd been great.

I led the way out of my room, my jumper back on and the sleeves carefully pulled down to hide my bloody bandage. I should check it soon, change it out. After dinner, perhaps.

Damian, Josh, and Mathilda were already seated, and they'd decked it for Caesar too. He either had to take the seat at the end of the table or next to Mathilda.

I veered between what would be the best choice for him, ultimately deciding on the one next to Mathilda, so I took the place at the end, Caesar on one side, Josh on the other.

"Everyone, this is Caesar." I motioned to him, then to all of them in turn. "Caesar, this is Damian, Josh, and my sister Mathilda."

They all were friendly enough in their greeting, though Josh seemed a bit absent and Mathilda kept shooting Caesar glances I couldn't decipher. I hoped she wasn't about to embarrass me.

"So what do you do for a living, Caesar?"

I narrowed my eyes at her, warning her to be nice, but she ignored me. Not that she wasn't being nice, because she sounded pleasant enough, I was just afraid of where she was going with it.

"I'm a piercer."

Riiight. I hadn't given much thought to his profession, but now he mentioned it again... I only had the one piercing and there was a certain one I'd had fleeting thoughts about getting.

"Piercer, really?"

Josh leaned over the table to grab the mug of lemonade—and my eyes zeroed in on where his sleeve involuntarily pulled up, revealing white gauze underneath instead of the scarred skin I'd grown used to seeing.

"I've always wanted a piercing, but when you're studying classical dance, it's not exactly acceptable to have one anywhere they show. Unless they're in your ears, anyway."

I drew my lower lip in between my teeth, worrying my lip ring. Josh had slipped up? He'd been harm-free for *months*, something he'd been very proud of. When had this happened? Surely not this weekend? When I'd been gone for two nights without a single word...

I lifted my gaze away from Josh's arm—which

was now busy pouring the lemonade into his glass—and found Damian watching me. A blush crept up my neck at being caught staring, and I bowed my head quickly.

"There's always *hidden* piercings," Caesar suggested and my head snapped up at that, because... well, because obviously, there weren't that many places you could hide a piercing on your body. Especially not while dancing in nothing but tight-fitting clothes that looked like a second skin.

Now I scowled at Mathilda for a whole different reason. She definitely wasn't getting herself a piercing in any hidden parts! I threw a glare at Caesar too, just to get my point across to them both, and he seemed to laugh back, even if he wasn't smiling.

Dinner went by in companionable silence.

Damian and Josh weren't that big on talking, or maybe they just didn't know what to say with another person at the table. Not that they were big conversationalists to begin with, but usually they were a bit more chatty.

Josh still seemed absent through the whole meal.

Mathilda didn't ask Caesar any dumb questions or tell him any embarrassing stories about me—so I counted that as a win.

"Thanks for the food." Caesar rinsed his plate and

put it in the dishwasher before I could protest that he was a guest and shouldn't have to do that. He only grinned at me as I threw him a scowl before rinsing my own.

"You're welcome." Josh smiled, but it was tight.

Caesar's grin faded a bit.

"Come on." I took his hand and dragged him with me back into my bedroom.

"I don't think they like me." He sunk down on my bed, dejected.

"I don't think it's you." I opened up my laptop. I hadn't shut it off the last time I'd used it, so the password screen came up right away. I logged in and clicked up a new tab on my browser, where I quickly typed in the URL to Josh's blog. He wrote *everything* on that blog. I'd made it a daily habit to read it, or at least a weekly one, it depended on how low my moods were.

"What're you doing?" He cocked his head curiously.

"Something's wrong." The blog loaded, but there wasn't a new post. Nothing new since last Wednesday. "Dammit."

"What is it?"

"Nothing. Well... Josh was out of sorts at dinner." I didn't like it when something was clearly wrong, especially when I didn't know what it was. "I'm just looking at his blog, but he hasn't written anything new."

Caesar didn't say anything.

I swivelled around on the chair so I could look at him. He did look dejected. "It's not you. Trust me, I know it wasn't you. Something's not right with Josh, and then Damian gets worried, and… well, the atmosphere around here isn't all that great then. Not that it normally is, but it's better than this."

I liked for things to be normal. I was terrified of anything changing.

There it is. The root of it.

Change…

My whole life had been turned on its head when my dad died. Not that anyone else would die, right? Surely Josh wasn't suicidal enough for that? Not anymore, at least? He had been in hospital before, and I suppose it had been because he'd been suicidal. Not that anyone had told me much back then—I'd been *too young*. "I saw his arm. It was bandaged, so—something's wrong."

"Matty." Caesar leaned over and took my hands in his, thumbs rubbing circles over the thin skin, over my knuckles. "Does he cut himself, too? Like you do?"

"He's been cutting most of his life. His arms… There isn't any undamaged skin anywhere, not on his forearms and not on his upper arms." I stared down at his hands squeezing mine. "First time I cut myself, I did it because I was curious. I'd seen Josh's arms, and I just wondered what it would be like—" I tried to dislodge the lump in my throat by swallowing, but it stuck with me, making my voice all hoarse. "It was so addictive and I continued doing it. And then... then Dad *died*. And then, Josh almost died, too. And everything went to hell with Mum. And now I can't stop."

"Do they know any of this? How you feel, what you do?"

I shook my head quickly.

"What about Josh? What does he do to help himself with his cutting and the likes?"

What I should be doing. "He goes to therapy."

"Why aren't you in therapy?"

"I don't want to go chat with some stranger." I was still staring at our hands. "I'm dealing with stuff on my own. It's fine."

"Matty, it's *not*." He let go of my hand to rest his lightly over my forearm, his touch feather-light. "This is proof you're not dealing."

I closed my eyes now, unable to face sitting there in front of him. Why was he being like this? Couldn't we just go back to bed, get naked again? It was so much better than *talking*. "Caesar… I don't want to talk about this."

I pulled away from him, scooting back on the bed, then lay down on my back before I opened my eyes again. I wished the stars would glow, so I had something interesting to watch. As it was now, they were almost the exact same colour as the ceiling.

Is he going to leave?

My chest squeezed tight at the thought. Even if I didn't want to talk, I didn't want him to leave me alone either.

He sighed, but he didn't leave. Instead he stretched out next to me so we lay shoulder to shoulder.

I held my breath, waiting for him to say something, but he didn't. So I fumbled for his hand, because it'd been good when he'd been holding both of mine earlier.

"I want things to stay the way they are," I mumbled. "I don't want anything to change. I don't want anyone else to die."

"Change doesn't have to mean that anyone dies."

"It might. Josh… Even if he is in therapy, he's struggling." Had been long before he'd ever met Damian. I probably didn't even know the half of what had happened to him.

Caesar squeezed my hand tight. "I want you to be okay, Matty."

The words, spoken in a low voice, did something to me, let something loose inside. I turned over, curled into his side. I didn't say anything else, I couldn't, and he didn't either.

CHAPTER 11

"Matt!"

I was on my way to the bathroom, but doubled back to face Mathilda, who stood in the kitchen doorway. "What?"

She held her phone out to me.

"Who is it?" I eyed it suspiciously.

"Mum wants to talk to you."

Hell no. "I'm busy." I turned away and headed over to the bathroom.

Mathilda's eyes narrowed. "What are you so busy with?"

"I'm going out." Over to Caesar's, to be more exact. But I wasn't about to say that to her so she could tell Mum. Mum had nothing to do with my life anymore.

"Matt." She didn't sound all that impressed with me. But then she had a good relationship with Mum —that Dad had died and Mum had changed completely didn't seem to faze her any.

I shut the door after me—didn't slam it, but shut it *resolutely*.

When I came out again Mathilda wasn't in the kitchen. She wasn't in the living room either, so no one stopped me on my way over to the front door.

Damian was at work, Josh was… out somewhere, I had no idea. Why Mathilda was around was beyond me, considering she was always so damn busy. Out with her mates, practicing dance even when she was on holiday, out shopping.

Where she got the money from was also beyond me, because she didn't have a job. Maybe Mum's new guy bought her affection. He certainly seemed the type.

Caesar was all bright and smiley when he opened the door to me. "Hey, Matty."

I let him drag me inside—and then shove me up against the door once he'd closed it. His lips ravished mine, kissing me to within an inch of my life.

Now this I can get used to.

"Hey," I breathed out when he eventually broke the kiss.

He leant his forehead against mine. "How're you feeling today?"

"Better." At least now I was here with him.

Something scraped against my thigh and I jumped backwards in surprise—hitting my head against the door. When I looked down, however, I saw it was just Caesar's dog. The dog I hadn't really greeted and whose name I didn't even know.

"Hey, there." I scratched her behind the ear. Her fur was coarse and curly, so different from Storm's long, straight, soft fur. "What's her name?"

"Molly." Caesar crouched down too and stroked down her back.

"What breed is she?" I knew nothing about dogs, except for my own.

"Poodle. Miniature size." He smiled proudly. "Did you know that poodles are the second most intelligent dog breed? They clock in right after border collies."

It was like a knife was stabbed into my heart. "I had a border collie."

He blinked. "You did?"

I nodded. "She died. She got sick, something with her liver, and Mum—she didn't think it was worth spending so much money when we didn't know if she'd get to live longer in the end." It had been the year after Dad died and Storm had been the only one I had, and then she'd been euthanised because Mum couldn't be arsed trying to save her. Just like she couldn't be arsed to consider her children in her new life.

"I'm sorry, Matty." His hand landed on my shoulder, squeezing gently.

"It's almost two years ago now." It had been almost as bad as losing Dad—and Mum too, though I was more bitter about her new priorities than anything else.

"You can always come and cuddle Molly if you need to," he offered, smiling kindly.

I managed a weak one in return. "Thanks." She was cute, with her black and curly fur. Her ears were fluffier than the rest of her and her eyes were wide and dark as she gazed up at me. "She's really cute."

He chuckled. "Sometimes I like to put some of her fur in a pink bow." He scooped up some coarse fur on the top of her head and wrapped his thumb and index finger around it to imitate a hairband. "When the fur's longer anyway. It's a little short now. But she's absolutely adorable with that little bow."

Yeah, I could only imagine. I'd never dolled Storm up, but she'd been cute enough without it. But I didn't want to talk about Storm or Mum or Dad or any of my personal shit. Not with Caesar. I liked being around him and I didn't want my issues to darken any of the good feelings he brought forth.

"So what're you up to?" I needed to change the subject.

"I just came home, actually. Went out for a walk with Molly right after work and now I thought I'd watch some porn."

A startled laugh left me. "Porn in the middle of the day?"

"Why not?" He grinned wickedly as he straightened up. "There are no rules about porn having to be enjoyed only at certain times."

Well, that was true. And I *did* like porn.

So we ended up on the sofa, both of us sprawled, and with twinks shagging loudly on his big screen. Of course we didn't watch the telly much, as we ended up doing some porn on our own. Thankfully, what we did together no one else could watch.

I stared down into his eyes as I rode him, moving slowly up and down his cock. He gripped my thighs, gaze locked with mine, lying there silently while he let me take the lead.

Something moved in the corner of my eye. I turned my head, but couldn't see anything. Maybe it had been Molly. I didn't know where she was right now.

I stared back down at Caesar, leaning forward

slightly so I could plant my hands against his chest. I rubbed my thumbs over his erect nipples, earning a light gasp from him.

"Nipple-piercings—" I started thoughtfully.

"What about them?"

I stopped moving, letting his dick stay buried inside me. "Are they worth it?"

His eyelids fluttered closed for a moment. "Yeah, people say so." His voice was strained. It was clear he'd rather get to the fucking instead of having this conversation.

But something had piqued my interest. "Who does?"

"Everyone who comes in the shop to get them," he clarified. "Or their partners. Or a couple of blokes I've been with who've had them. Makes the nipples even more tender, they say, and it's awesome."

I pinched his nipples lightly for mentioning other blokes now he was right in the middle of sex with me —earning me a louder gasp this time around—then I finally started to move again. "I want one."

"Ahh—one what?" His neck flushed and he couldn't lie still anymore. His hips started bucking under me, meeting me on each upstroke as I sat down on him.

"A nipple piercing." I braced my hands properly on his chest and upped my speed. My thighs burned, not used to this position, but it was a kind of burn that was necessary to receive the pleasure his dick brought me.

"Really?" He sounded faintly surprised. Or maybe he was just close to coming and couldn't imagine I would bring this up right now.

"Yeah." I straightened back up, braced one hand on the back of the sofa while the other fisted my cock. If he was about to come I wasn't about to be far behind.

"Ahh—yeah," he groaned, staring at my flushed dick through heavy-lidded eyes. "Come on my chest, Matty."

I planned on it—and I did.

"Yes, just like that." He stared down at his stomach, at the white, sticky puddles.

Now it was his turn. I moved faster, clenching around him. A long, drawn-out moan left him, his head tilting back, baring his throat... and then he came too.

I rose up enough that his dick slipped out of me, then I collapsed on him and attacked his lips, pushing my tongue past them, kissing him deeply.

Something resembling a scream came from the TV and I turned my head to stare at the two blokes right in the midst of their own orgasm.

"That's a loud one," Caesar murmured, hands

stroking down my back, over my arse, and then squeezing it.

"I hope I don't make sounds like that." I ground my hips, and my flaccid, sticky dick against his groin. He still wore the condom and we should probably get up and be rid of it.

"Nah. You're pretty quiet, actually." He brushed his lips over my neck.

"So about that nipple piercing…"

"You really want one?"

"Yeah." I rubbed my nose over his collarbone. "I do."

He chuckled, squeezing my arse harder, slipping one finger down the crack to tease. "Then I'll do it."

"Soon," I added.

"Very soon." He grinned. "I'll check tomorrow when I've got time and I'll text you."

That sounded good. And with that out of mind for now… "Want to take a shower together?"

His lips stretched into a wry grin. "Would we get much showering done?"

"Probably not." I climbed off his lap and stood on wobbly legs on the floor. *Damn*, but riding him like that sure wasn't something I was used to.

He laughed as he stood up behind me, shoving me lightly. "Need me to hold you up?"

I only grabbed his hand and dragged him to the bathroom with me. What I had planned for the shower was sure to shut him up.

CHAPTER 12

*H*ere I was, sitting in a leather chair, with my shirt off. My nipples had puckered right up in the chilly air inside, and Caesar was readying his stuff. I didn't know what it was called—maybe something as simple as a needle, because it sure looked like one.

"You absolutely sure about this, Matty?" He didn't look at me as he asked, busy with whatever preparation he was doing.

"Yeah." I sat up straighter as Caesar wheeled his chair over. "It'll hurt, right?"

"Not going to lie to you, love—*yes*, it hurts." He gave me a wry, apologetic grin. "But everyone says it's worth it."

I wasn't a stranger to pain. My razor blade and I

were quite good mates, after all. And I did have my lip-piercing, so it wasn't like this was my first time around the block. Still, it was my *nipple*. It felt like such a bigger thing than cutting up my arms or having a ring through my lip. This was something *intimate*.

I wondered what he was thinking as he bent in close. Two days ago, he'd been sucking and nibbling on them both eagerly. *I wonder if he gets to see a lot of half-naked blokes. Very likely. Probably completely naked ones too.* There were such a thing as genital piercings, but that... was taking it too far.

Caesar straightened up with a laugh. "What are you shuddering about?"

I didn't even know I'd been shuddering. "Thinking about genital piercings."

He quirked one eyebrow in question. "Want one of those as well?"

"Hell no!" *Definitely not.*

"I don't know, I think a PA is pretty rad. Been thinking about getting one of those for myself."

I sat there like a question mark. "A PA?"

"Prince Albert?" His brow quirked up further, and I could swear he was amused now.

I shrugged, still clueless.

"It's a piercing through your cock. The urethra and the underside of it."

Oh. Yes, I'd seen those. In porn, mostly. Big-arsed ring on big-arsed penises. I swallowed. "You seen many cocks like that?"

"Oh yeah." He grinned wickedly. "Done plenty of those, I have."

I wasn't sure if there was a double-meaning to his words. Obviously he'd pierced many of them, but had he actually had sex with a lot of blokes who had them too? I didn't dare ask. Wasn't sure I wanted to hear the answer—especially not if it was in the affirmative.

"You want one, huh? Why haven't you got one then?" He was in an excellent position to get new piercings, considering he worked with people doing them.

"Well, there's the healing process, where you can't have sex. Kind of makes me falter, you know." He leaned back in, his tools or needles or whatever they were called held at the ready.

I sucked in a breath, intending to hold it until he'd finished.

"Try to relax, Matty. It'll be better that way."

Relax, yeah, as if that was easy with that big-arsed needle so close to my nipple.

It stung, I wasn't going to lie about it. But at the same time, it wasn't so different from my cutting, either, in its intensity. When I cut deep, it could hurt even more than this.

"There you go then." When I opened my eyes, Caesar had sat back. He was grinning at me now, eyes twinkling. "Was it bad?"

"Not really. I expected worse." I looked down at my bare chest, at the sore nipple that now had a ring through it. "This is amazing." I meant it wholeheartedly. Getting it done had been a quick decision, but not one I was going to regret anytime soon, I was confident about that.

He chuckled, then set about cleaning up after himself. I, meanwhile, carefully pulled my T-shirt and jumper back on. Both were loose, so it shouldn't be much of a problem for my new piercing.

Once he was done, I followed him back out to the counter so I could pay.

"Since you're you, you'll get a discount." He winked at me.

"No, really—" He didn't have to do that. I was more than happy to pay in full.

He waved me away as he punched something in on the till. "Don't mention it, Matty. Here you go."

I paid by card, got a receipt, and then I took a step back to allow the person who had come up behind me to take my place. Caesar stood at the counter still, even with his boss coming up. "Hey, mate, you all right?"

Caesar only blinked once, then shook his head, swaying.

"Get away from the counter, mate." His boss steered him away, standing him right in the middle of the floor.

What's going on? I made to take a step forward when Caesar suddenly dropped with a *thunk*, then started to jerk around on the floor. His boss pulled off his jumper, bunched it up and put it under his head, but he didn't touch him.

"What's wrong with him?" I was back around the counter now, staring down at him as he continued to jerk.

Caesar's boss didn't answer because he was on the phone. I heard the words *seizure, ambulance* and *hurry. This can't be good!* I wanted to crouch down, to touch him, speak to him, but his boss had stayed clear so maybe I should too.

The jerking stopped. Caesar's whole body seemed to sag—and then it started up again.

"Bloody hell!" His boss yelled, then pressed the phone he was still on closer to his ear. "He's having another one! Get here *now*!"

I couldn't help myself. Fuck the fact that he

stayed clear, I wasn't going to. So I crouched down next to him, putting my hand on his chest.

"Don't try to restrain him!"

Oh no, no, no. Caesar! I didn't know how much time went by. All I knew was that he was jerking, the seizure stopped, only to start up again almost immediately. Then the ambulance crew was there, with a trolley they put his seizing body on.

"I'm his boyfriend," I told them in a panic as they started out of the shop with him. "Let me come with him, please!"

One of them nodded and I wasted no time jumping into the back of the ambulance. My whole body trembled as I sank down, but not nearly as violently as Caesar was still jerking. The paramedic yelled something to the one who sat in the driver's seat up front but I couldn't understand the medical terms. All my focus was on Caesar.

The seizure stopped, only to start up again. I curled in on myself as I watched it happen. *Not him, no!* I put my hands in front of my face as the paramedic did something to him, then yelled some more to the driver.

I rocked back and forth on the uncomfortable seat, seeing nothing but Caesar's pale—turning slightly blue now—face as he continued to jerk.

I can't lose him. No! Not him too!

∽

"MATT, COME ON."

Damian's hands squeezed my shoulders, but I shrugged him off. Tears streamed down my face and my hands were clenched so tightly I must be losing circulation in them. But none of that mattered, because Caesar was on that bed and he was still seizing up.

Damian grabbed me again, harder this time. I tried to shrug him off again, but he wouldn't have it. "We have to let them work on him. Come on, let's go out in the hall."

I shook my head, eyes blurry but fastened on Caesar. The monitor started beeping loudly and everyone exploded into action, even if they'd all been moving around frantically before.

I know what that means. I know what it means. I'd heard Damian talk about his work. I'd seen all the medical dramas on the telly… Caesar's heart was giving out and now they were all scrambling to get it beating again. I saw the machine, saw the paddles handed to one of the doctors—

I was screaming and Damian's arms were round my waist, dragging me out of the room, away from the line on the screen. *If that line goes flat…* I cried and yelled and kicked out, but Damian held on, wrangling me down into one of the uncomfortable plastic chairs outside.

"Matt! Take a deep breath." He was crouched in front of me now, hands still on my trembling shoulders, holding me down.

I shook my head violently. "I c-c-can't!" I cried, deep, body-wrenching sobs escaping me. "Y-you have t-to h-h-help him! I c-can't l-l-lose him t-too!" *I've lost too many people!* I bent over, burying my face in my hands, but the sobbing didn't die out. If anything, it increased. And it *hurt*. "D-dad a-a-a-and S-St-Storm—" I couldn't continue. The rest of the sentence was lost in my sobs. They were dead and now Caesar was on the verge of dying, and *why was everyone dying?* Couldn't everyone just *live*?

"Matt, try to breathe. You have to *breathe*." Damian sounded a bit panicked now, but I wasn't sure that was because of me, because Dad and my dog were dead, or because of Caesar.

"I c-can't!" I whimpered, arms falling down to clutch my midsection. Everything hurt. Speaking hurt, crying hurt, *breathing* hurt.

Damian stood up, turning away from me, and that hurt too. *Is he giving up on me?* I hadn't exactly been the best person to deal with. So depressed I couldn't move out of bed at times, still refusing to get help, cutting myself... But now I had something that made me happy—being around Caesar made me bloody *happy* and now that was going to be taken away from me too, like everything else had been.

"Bring me a trolley!" That was Damian. *Why does he need a trolley?*

He walked off, uncaring of my sobs as they increased and I fell sideways, resting my forehead against the arm of the chair. I couldn't stop crying, sobbing, *hurting*— I just wanted it to stop!

A trolley was wheeled in front of me by a nurse in scrubs, and then Damian was back too. Somehow, they both managed to get me on that bed, because I certainly wasn't capable of moving at all.

Damian rolled up my sleeve, and then a needle was stuck into the blood vessel in the crook of my elbow. I didn't even feel it. Everything hurt so much already, a syringe stuck into me did little difference. I didn't know what it was he inserted at first, but then I felt my body calm down, start to relax, and I managed to stop crying, the sobbing eased—and then I fell into blackness.

CHAPTER 13

I blinked my eyes open, feeling both heavy and disoriented. I was lying down and when I managed to get my neck to lift, I saw I was stretched out on a bed. In a dark room.

Everything came back in flashes and my blood ran cold as I remembered the loud, shrieking *beep* of the monitor as Caesar went into arrest. I drew a sharp breath, which caused motion at my side.

When I turned my head that way, I found Damian leaning forward to look at me. "Feeling better?"

I tried to nod, but turning my head his way had been too much. "Yeah. Caesar?" I had to know. Better to find out right away then lie and wonder about it. *Please let him be all right.*

"He's stable." Damian stood from the chair he'd been sitting in and came to perch on the edge of my bed. "He's going to be fine."

I fumbled for his hand, which he had braced against the mattress. I needed to hold onto something and it was the only thing there. Damian let me hold it, let me clutch at it, and he just sat there as he watched my face in the dim light.

"Really?" I couldn't quite believe it. His heart had *stopped*, hadn't it? Wasn't that what those *beeps* on the machine meant?

"Yeah. Really."

I drew in a shaky breath in relief, but my eyes still filled with tears. They trickled slowly down my cheeks. "I was so afraid," I whispered brokenly. "Last time I was here it was Dad. I was so afraid that Caesar would—"

"But he didn't," he interrupted. "He didn't. He's fine."

I managed a nod then, as if I needed to do it to reassure myself. "What was wrong with him?"

"He has epilepsy. Tonic-clonic seizures." Upon my blank look, he added, "You might've heard of the older term, grand mal?"

I nodded again, hesitant. "Is it chronic?"

He tipped his head down for a second before

meeting my gaze again. "Yeah. Epilepsy is a chronic disease of the brain, but there are good medicines nowadays. Many people live next to normal lives with their epilepsy."

"But he can die from it?" I couldn't get the sound of that bloody machine out of my head.

"You can die from anything." He was being as realistic as ever.

I took a shuddering breath now. "He'll be fine?"

"Yes, Matt. This was a particularly severe seizure. Or seizures, as you saw. Normally, a seizure lasts under five minutes and doesn't need medical attention. Just a lot of rest. If it does last over five minutes, or if there are repeated seizures, such as he had today, then medical attention is needed immediately. I talked to his doctor, and I read his chart, and it seems he doesn't normally have that many seizures anymore."

"What triggers them?" I wanted to know. I needed to know. I hoped it wasn't anything I'd done. Maybe too much sex? We were constantly all over each other, after all. It must be exhausting for him.

"Triggers are different from person to person. Alcohol and drugs are generally a bad idea though, as they lower seizure control."

Alcohol. "Caesar was drinking the night we met.

We finished the bottle he had with him, and when we got back to his place we mixed Vodka half and half."

Damian frowned. "That's generally *not* a good idea for someone who's epileptic. Not for someone who isn't, either, for that matter."

"He hasn't had anything to drink since though." I didn't think so, anyway. I felt I needed to defend him too, even if the thought of all that alcohol consumption that night scared me now I knew what it could lead to. Caesar was never going to be touching a drink again, that much was certain.

"Does he take his medicine?"

"I don't know. I've never seen him take anything." I shrugged helplessly. But then I'd only stayed with Caesar for the weekend—I'd only got to know him. Still, we'd got so close so fast... "Why would he keep this from me?"

"I don't know, Matt. You'd have to ask him."

I turned my head away from him now as feelings I'd kept buried deep down came bubbling up to the surface. "I never told Dad. Not Mum either." Not that I felt like talking to her, lately.

"Told them what?"

"That I'm gay." Guilt gnawed inside me, so big it was like it was going to consume me whole.

"You shouldn't let that bother you, Matt. Ray would've loved you, no matter what. You know that." He didn't mention Mum. We never really talked about Mum lately.

"But it's something he should've known. *I've* known for years, and still I never told anyone. It's too late now. He'll *never* know." I should've told them, both of them, when I figured it out, back when I was thirteen. I should've been more open with them, not shut them out. "How did *you* tell them?"

"I never really did." Damian's voice was low, quiet. "They stopped by the flat to visit me one day, Josh was there... and they just knew. They asked us both to come to dinner. They never did tell me what tipped them off, though I reckon Josh coming out of my bedroom was a big clue."

I pushed myself up into more of a sitting position, drawing my knees up to hug them. "You think they just knew about me too? Even if I never told them?"

"They were perceptive. It wouldn't surprise me."

I liked the sound of that. "I miss Dad. I miss him so much. Will it ever go away?" As for Mum... *She buggered off on a month-long honeymoon with her new bloke. Good riddance, really.*

"No." At least he was honest. "But it'll be easier, with time."

I realised with a start that Damian knew exactly what he was talking about. He hadn't just lost *my* dad, his uncle, but he'd lost his entire family. His mum and dad, his sisters... they were all dead. It was never something I thought about, because I'd grown up with Damian around. He was more of a brother than a cousin. But he *did* know, what it was like. He'd been all alone; if it hadn't been for my parents, he wouldn't have had *anyone*.

"Ready to go home?" His hand squeezed my knee. "It's late. I think it's best if you get some rest in your own bed."

"Caesar... Can't I stay with him?" Fuck my bed. My boyfriend—if that was what he was—had almost died.

He shook his head. "Only family's allowed. Besides, he needs his rest too. Come home, and we'll come back tomorrow morning during visiting hours."

I didn't want to. I ached to see Caesar, to touch him and to hold him and make sure he really was alive and well, but I knew I wouldn't be allowed. It hurt inside to admit it, but it was true. So I nodded and left the bed behind as I followed Damian outside.

They didn't own a car, Damian and Josh, but he led me over to one now. I recognised it upon closer inspection as Josh's mother's car. I was grateful he'd borrowed it, because taking a bus or the tube in my condition right now... it wasn't something I thought I could do.

I was silent on the ride home, thoughts swirling. Damian didn't say anything either. Not until we were back in the flat and I moved towards my bedroom door. "Goodnight, Matt."

I looked over my shoulder at him. I was thankful that Damian had been there tonight, that he'd been available when I'd got to A&E and frantically asked a nurse to page him. He'd taken care of me, had sedated me and sat with me, and then explained everything to me. "Goodnight, Damian."

I trudged into my room, shutting the door firmly behind me. My bed wasn't made, it was all rumpled, and I fell down into the mess of it, burying my face in my pillow. Only two days ago Caesar had been here, all happy and seductive and comforting. And now I was alone while he was in the hospital...

I fumbled for my journal, which was lying all out in the open on the bedside table. The pencil was jammed into the book, on the next available page, and I grabbed it, writing like I was possessed.

Sadness
A blurred world
Too slow, too fast
never stopping

A bed, a duvet
it's black
My tomb
Life's too hard
to face

Once I finished, I flipped one page back to read what I'd written two days ago, after Caesar had left. It had been a good day, even after my worry about Josh... Caesar had managed to cheer me up, and I hadn't really given it much thought since.

Bodies —
pressed together
An intricate dance
Pleasure —
all-consuming
Addiction
Born

I was addicted, all right. To Caesar, to his smile, his touch, his skin, his dick... Everything about him was addictive—and he made me feel better about myself. When I was with him, things weren't so bleak, so heavy, so *difficult*.

With him I could let lose, enjoy myself, enjoy what we had and what we did together. He was warm, caring, funny, great in bed… and he'd almost died.

Die, dying, dead. Dad had been dead for three years now. I couldn't even remember what that day had been like, before I'd gone off to college. Before I'd come home to find the police and the fire engine and Josh unconscious on the kitchen floor with blood around him, and then Dad's wrecked car…

I could remember all of that in great detail. I couldn't remember words though, what they'd said to each other, what had been said to me. And I couldn't remember what it'd been like before I'd headed off to school.

Had it been something nice? Or had I been distant, depressed, like I'd been long before Dad died? Had my last words to him been something *unkind*? Had I been angry with him? Or had I been too busy with myself and my dark thoughts and feelings?

I hated that I couldn't remember. That day was a blur. The days following it were a blur.

A tentative knock on my door broke my chain of depressive thoughts. "Matt? Can I come in?"

Josh. "Y-yeah." I hadn't locked the door, so I didn't have to get up and open it. Still, it wouldn't do to lie down, so I scooted up into a sitting position, arranging the duvet over my crossed legs.

Josh came inside, closing the door softly behind him, then he sat down on my desk chair. "I'm sorry about today."

"Yeah." Today had started out so good, so promising, only to end up a cluster-fuck of Caesar almost dying and me being so hysterical I had to be sedated. I hadn't even cried when my dad *died*, yet today...

"How are you doing?" His gaze, a startling, brilliant green, rested on me. Worried, curious, anxious; a mix of everything.

"Not so good." I couldn't lie and say I was good, like I tended to do, because *no one* would feel good after going through what I had today.

"I'm so sorry." Josh bent forward, his elbows resting on his knees. He was wearing a long-sleeved jumper, so the skin on his arms was out of sight. "I'm so sorry you had to experience that, that you had to go through it. You didn't deserve that."

A lump threatened to form in my throat and I swallowed heavily to try and be rid of it. It didn't work. "I reacted worse today than I did when my own dad died. What does that say about me?"

Josh lifted a startled gaze to meet mine again. "You were in denial. Or at least that's what Vincent said was most likely."

I ran a hand over my face. "You talk to your

psychologist about me?" I didn't know what to feel about that.

"Of course I do. I tell him everything and he helps me figure out what I feel about it, and help me make sense of it all." Josh had always been very open about going to therapy and how much it helped him. If I ever went to see a therapist, I didn't think I'd ever manage to be so open about it. "Maybe today— when you saw that he was crashing— maybe that's when you realised it."

"Realised what?" I'd realised a lot of things. That he was about to die and that I didn't want him to die, that I cared about him too much to lose him.

"That he's never coming back."

I frowned. "I've always known Dad wasn't ever coming back." Being dead made sure of that.

"Yeah, but— you've been shut down ever since it happened, ever since he died." Josh's gaze flittered to the floor. "Today the feelings you've kept buried came back to the surface. You reacted very close to how Mathilda reacted at the hospital, or so Damian said. Crying, hysterical… Today you finally got to grieve, Matt."

I tried to blink the tears away, but it only resulted in them falling down my cheeks. "I didn't cry once. Not the night they told me, not the days following, not the funeral—" I covered my face with my palms, not wanting him to see just how many tears were welling up and flowing over. "I'm the worst son ever."

"You're not." I heard my chair roll over the floor, and then Josh's hand was on my upper arm, squeezing gently.

"I am! I cried more for a bloke I've only known for a few days than I ever did for my own dad." I bent over so far, I could nearly rest my hands and face against my still-crossed legs.

"You were in shock back then, Matt. Your dad— it happened so unexpectedly. It shouldn't have happened at all, but it did, and no one ever saw it coming. Claire and Mathilda grieved—you were in shock. Both reactions are just as normal, so you shouldn't blame yourself like that, you shouldn't feel so guilty." His arm inched around my upper back, hugging me. "What happened today, with your bloke... It was a traumatic experience. Everyone would've reacted. You reacted perhaps a bit more than most would've, because you've lost someone before, Matt. You've been in shock and today that was blown apart by someone else you care about almost dying."

I sniffled, trying to dry the tears, but more kept on trickling, so there was really no point.

"What we've been asking you ever since it

happened, about going to therapy… We still think you should. You've been keeping everything locked up for so long, and the past year hasn't been good years for you. So Matt, if you think it's hard, therapy *does* help. It really does."

"No." I shook my head violently. I didn't want to talk to a stranger. I didn't want to talk to anyone. Talking wouldn't make *anything* better.

I heard Josh sigh, but he didn't press the issue anymore. Instead he just rubbed his hand over my back, which was kind of soothing.

"Caesar's fine. I'll be fine." Well, as fine as I could be, anyway. I should take them up on the offer, on therapy, but I couldn't. Even if I did go to see someone, what would I say? I didn't know how to explain my feelings, they were all a jumbled mess. *I* was a mess. I'd rather just stay with Caesar, because he made me feel alive again.

"If you change your mind, you know we're always here."

Josh left the room when I didn't say anything else, and I curled up on my side. As I stared at the empty desk chair, I held my hands close to my chest. And then I realised—

Damian had *sedated* me. I clearly remembered through the hysteria that he'd rolled up my sleeve.

"Oh no." I drew a shaky breath, terror coursing through me.

They know.

Josh had seen me before, back before Dad died, but it hadn't been so bad then. Now, however…

Damian knows.

CHAPTER 14

*W*alking down the corridors was a special kind of hell. Not just because I didn't know what was awaiting me at the end of them, but also because I'd done this walk before. Not in these exact corridors, but hospital corridors were mostly the same.

The door to Caesar's room was wide open. I approached it slowly, hesitant. My stomach was in knots, my chest tight. I had difficulty breathing.

First thing I noticed was how the sun shone in through the big windows, lighting up the whole, sterile room. Caesar's parents—or his mother, at least, and a man I assumed was his dad—stood by it. The man was looking outside, his mother was facing her son.

Caesar was on the bed, his chest rising and falling, his eyes open. He had a far-away look on his face, as if he was in deep thought, but he blinked as he registered my uncomfortable movements. A smile spread on his lips, and suddenly it was like all the breath was knocked out of me.

"Matty."

I stared at him. He wasn't his usual energetic self, he seemed knackered and out of it. The blaring sound of the machine flashed through my mind and I saw how the line started spiking.

And then I heard nothing but silence. A body, a trolley, pale and unmoving and *dead*. Dad's face bruised, the bleeding that must've been there washed away. His chest... it didn't rise and fall. He was silent, all was silent.

A shaking breath escaped my lips. I'd lain in bed all night thinking I could handle it, handle being with Caesar because I *desperately* wanted to be near him, but he had nearly *died*. He *had* died, his heart had stopped, but they'd been able to bring him back. My dad hadn't been so lucky, he'd succumbed, and what if next time Caesar wasn't so lucky either? What if next time—

Mathilda's screams rang through my head.

I took a step back. I registered Caesar's stricken expression, but I *couldn't*.

You're going the wrong way! A voice screamed inside, right alongside Mathilda's screams upon seeing the truth with her own eyes. The truth she'd insisted upon seeing.

Go to him! I couldn't. Dad *had* died, Storm was dead, Caesar almost. He could still die. And I wasn't numb anymore, not by a long shot. I was terrified.

So all I could do was turn on my heels and run.

I FELL to my knees in front of the grave. Last time I'd been there, there'd still been a massive pile of dirt and only a white cross in the ground to show it was actually Dad's grave. Now the ground was flat and green and he had a proper gravestone.

I can't believe I haven't been here since the funeral. Three bloody years!

We'd been supposed to be here together, all of us, that day the headstone had been put there. I'd refused. I'd stayed at home, buried in my bed, my arms and thighs bleeding. It was two and a half years ago now.

I really am the worst son.

"Dad." Tears streamed in endless torrents from my eyes and I couldn't do anything to stop them. The dam had been breached, and now it was all over-flowing.

I was alone, as far as I could see there wasn't anyone else visiting loved ones. No one else was poking around the cemetery, at least not anywhere near me.

My hands were braced on the grass, my fingers clenching around the tufts. "Dad… *Dammit!*" I ripped several tufts up and threw them. Not that they went far.

It wasn't fair. He shouldn't be dead. He shouldn't have left me all alone. He shouldn't have left Mum, messed her up so much I didn't even recognise her anymore. Left her to marry some tosser. I shouldn't have run away from Caesar when all I wanted was to curl up next to him, to hug him and kiss him and just *hold* him, to make sure he was all right.

"*Dad.*" I stared at the gold inscription spelling out his name, birth and date of death. "I'm gay. I n-never told you that. I don't know why. I just never d-did." A sob escaped me. "I'm so s-sorry." I didn't know what I was sorry for. For not telling him? For being gay in the first place? For never coming to visit after the funeral? "It's all messed up now. So bloody messed up."

I sat down on my bum and drew my knees up to hug tightly against my chest. It might be warm in the air, but the grass was damp, so it must've been raining during the night. My jeans sucked the wetness right up, though, but for the moment I couldn't bring myself to care.

"Why did you have to go and die?" I knew I was being unfair, that it wasn't *his* fault that he was dead. It had been Josh's stepfather. The git. He hadn't meant to do it... He'd only been after Josh. But he had rammed his car into Dad's, and while he'd walked away almost unscathed, Dad had *died*.

I wanted him to be here, alive and well. I wanted everything to go back to the way it had used to be. Things hadn't been perfect then either, I'd still been depressed and still been cutting myself, but at least Mum and Dad had been there for me. Even if they hadn't known, they'd been around. They'd been happy.

I hadn't appreciated it back then, but I did now. I just wanted him to *be* here.

I buried my face against my kneecaps as I cried. Caesar must hate me now. He certainly wouldn't want anything to do with me anymore. *I* didn't really want to have anything to do with myself anymore.

I'd panicked back there, in the hospital, when the images and the sounds and the lack of sounds, had come back to me. I hadn't *processed* Dad's death and then I'd been slapped right across the face with the possibility of Caesar's. I *cared* about Caesar and I couldn't lose him, like I'd lost Dad. Like Storm had been taken from me. I couldn't lose anyone else, not a single person more.

Caesar had been *fine* though. He'd looked tired and rough around the edges, but he'd been fine. I had, likely, seen to the fact that I would lose him anyway by pulling the shitty stunt I had.

"I know life's hard right now. I just want you to know that I'm here for you." Those had been Adam's words from over three years ago. Funny how most of the things from back then were blurry, but his words stood out to me even now, so long after he'd said them. *"I know what you're going through. I know it isn't easy."* Yeah, he would know, wouldn't he? Adam had lost both of his parents. In a sense, I had too, because while Mum was still alive, we had minimal contact. *"But if you do find you need someone to talk to, I'm always here."* I hadn't ever taken him up on that offer, though we'd been proper mates ever since.

My fingers came back wet after wiping at my tears, and I wiped them off again on my jeans. I stared at the gold inscription again, my chest tightening painfully.

I hated it. Hated that he was gone, hated the way I felt right now, hated myself for being such a coward. Both towards my parents, for not telling them the truth, and for running away from the one person who'd made me feel alive in over *three years*. I hated the look I'd seen on Caesar's face—and most of all I hated myself for putting it there.

I pushed up on my feet. The back of my thighs and my bum were wet, as were my knees. I shivered, not so much from the air, since that was warm, but from an inner chill. Wrapping my arms around myself didn't help much.

"I love you, Dad." I hadn't ever told him that. Maybe when I was a little kid, but once I grew up, became a depressed, self-harming teenager, it'd been below me to ever say those words to anyone. Fresh tears leaked from my eyes again and now I couldn't be bothered doing anything about them. I simply turned and walked away, arms still wrapped around myself and with my head bent.

I must look horrible all cried out, but I couldn't stop the crying either, so a bent head was as much privacy as I could get. They kept coming, the tears, kept trickling heavily down my cheeks, and it was a good thing I wasn't wearing any eyeliner because if I had there'd be black tracks all over my face by now.

I didn't know how long I walked for, but I came to my destination eventually. I looked up at the house where the flat I was seeking lay, and I took a deep breath before I went over to ring the doorbell.

It was Nick who opened the door. Tall, immaculately dressed, dark-haired, *proper* Nick. "Matt?" He was surprised to see me, but it quickly smoothed into worry as he took in my appearance.

"I-is Adam in?" I was shuddering from head to foot, likely from both the crying and the fact that my jeans were soaked through. *Please let him be in.*

Nick nodded and stepped back, allowing me to come inside. "Adam!" He helped me off with my jacket, hanging it up on the wall carefully. I let him do as he wished, too wet and shell-shocked to do anything myself.

"What?" Footsteps announced Adam's arrival seconds before he appeared in the hallway. His curious expression shifted into surprise as he looked me over, and then to worry. "Hey, Matt."

I wiped at my cheeks with stiff fingers, taking a shaking breath to try and calm myself. I didn't really know why I was there, what I was supposed to do, but Adam was the one who could maybe understand how I was feeling right now, so here I was.

"Come on, Matt." Adam was at my side, one arm wrapping around my shoulders as he led me further into the flat, out of the hallway.

"Get him out of those clothes so he won't get sick," Nick instructed as he followed us. He pointed to my jeans for emphasis.

"Yeah." Adam nodded to him, then led me into their bedroom. He sat me down on the edge of their bed, and I watched as Adam headed over to the closet. "Joggers okay? My jeans will be too big for you."

"Yeah, sure." I wiped at my eyes again, wishing for all the world the tears would just *stop*.

"What've you been up to?" Adam crossed back over to me. "You're cold, shivering, and *soaked*. Been raining in your part of town?"

"I was at Dad's grave," I admitted in a low voice, glancing at the joggers in Adam's hands. They looked rather nice and comfy. I undid the buttons on my skinny jeans and inched them down my thighs. They felt like they were glued to me, like I had to peel them off, and I breathed out in relief as I finally managed to yank them off my ankles. I took the joggers from Adam, saw his eyes on my thighs— instantly realising he wasn't watching me for the pleasure of it—and pulled them on as quickly as I could, leaving my own wet jeans in a puddle on the floor.

"Matt—"

"Adam, don't."

He stared at me, then sighed and sat down next to me. "Want to talk about it?"

"No. Not really." What would I say? I didn't know what I felt myself.

"Okay then." Adam lay down on the bed and stretched out.

I stared down at him, surprised he'd let it drop just like that, then followed his example and lay back too. I didn't want to talk, and even though the silence between us wasn't all that uncomfortable, I found myself starting to talk anyway. "What did you do when your parents died?"

"We lived up in Newcastle. When they died, my grandmother came up there and got us, Les and I, and took us back down to London with her."

"What about a funeral?"

"They're buried here." Adam smiled sadly up at the ceiling. "Mum grew up here, and dad had no other family, so they're buried here in London. We go to see them on their birthdays, their wedding anniversary and the date of their deaths. Sometimes I go just because I want to be near them."

"That's nice." I wasn't so sure if it was, but it *sounded* nice. I certainly hadn't got much out of visiting my Dad's grave just now, except a whole lot of crying.

"It's calming," Adam supplied in a low voice. "I don't really believe in anything supernatural, but sometimes it feels like… I don't know, like they're there watching me or something." He chuckled and dragged a hand through his hair. "Sounds silly, I know, especially as I don't believe in it, but there you have it."

"I didn't feel that." I frowned, then turned my attention back to Adam. He truly was gorgeous. I couldn't decide which one was better looking; Adam or Caesar. It would've been so much easier if Adam was available, if we could've been a thing. Adam didn't have a condition that could stop his heart, that could kill him.

"Matt?" He looked at me now, his blue eyes searching.

I couldn't continue crushing on Adam. He was my mate, he was spoken for, and… so was I now. "I haven't been to his grave before. Not since the funeral. I didn't go when they got the proper grave-stone. I just— I couldn't face it." I rubbed my hands together. They felt cold, numb, like they did in winter if I went out without gloves.

"You're shaking." Adam's hand, big and strong, reached over to me, gripping both of mine. His grip was warm and soothing.

I drew in a breath and slowly released it, then turned my head only to find myself mesmerised by those blue eyes. *Adam's safe.* Caesar had been safe. It had felt so good losing myself in him, and now—now he was in the hospital after having nearly died.

Tears started trickling again as a sob escaped me. I squeezed my eyes shut, hoping to stop them, but it didn't help.

Adam rolled over and hugged me tight. "Oh, Matt."

I clutched at him as I once again was overtaken by the tears and the grief and the shock and the big black hole that was depression. Had it really only been a day since I had my nipple pierced, since I'd been feeling happier than I had in a long time, ever since Dad died? It seemed such a long time ago now, and yet everything was so recent.

My dad... he'd died in that hospital. The exact same hospital I'd been in yesterday, the one where Caesar had nearly died. Hospitals equalled *death*—only not all the time, because Caesar had *lived*. So had Josh, back then, but it had looked bad for a while. He'd been in a coma for days.

"I don't m-mean to be such a m-mess."

"It's entirely understandable." His cheek rested against my tearstained one, his lips only inches from my ear.

You only know half of it. If I'd been normal, if I hadn't been this majorly depressed human being... I shouldn't have to be such a mess over three *years* after my dad died. But seeing Caesar struggling yesterday— it had brought something out in me. Maybe like Josh had said, I'd been in shock, and now it was all blown apart.

"It'll get better, eventually." Adam pulled away now and slowly sat up. He braced one hand on the bed and turned his body so that he still faced me. His gaze was worried. "Everyone grieves differently, that's what they all told me way back when. It's still a shock to have someone as important as your parents ripped away so suddenly without no warning. It's difficult to move past it, to move on. It's the most difficult thing you can ever do."

I sniffled and wiped at my cheeks. Losing Dad, having to bury him before I was even of age myself… it wasn't right, it wasn't fair, it was *cruel*. To find just a smidgeon of happiness again, now that was a surprise, only to have it ripped away by a beeping machine as the doctors tried to keep the heart beating… that was cruel too. I was back at square one. Alone, miserable, grieving. A proper mess.

And this wasn't the right way to go about dealing with things. This wasn't what I needed.

"I have to go." I sat up, not looking at him.

"You just got here." He moved and in the next second he'd gripped my hand, squeezing it tight.

I let him, for a few heartbeats—I might've even

squeezed back a little, but then I stood up. "I know. I'm sorry. I just— I have to go." I glanced back over my shoulder, saw him gaze at me in confusion. "Thanks for the joggers. I'll get them back to you." I exited the bedroom before I could make even more of a mess of myself.

I didn't see Nick, for which I was eternally grateful. Adam had followed me though and he loomed in the doorway as I quickly pulled my jacket and shoes on.

"Take care, Matt. You can come to me anytime, no matter what."

"Thanks." I had now—but I wasn't sure I would again.

I left. I had planned on going home. But it was so easy to stop by Boots, to buy the one thing I needed right now, and then to find a public toilet to lock myself in and do exactly what I'd been craving.

CHAPTER 15

Obviously the day had to come sometime. The day I cut too deep. The day I had to show up at the A&E, ashamed and cried out and with cuts so deep they wouldn't stop bleeding.

"Please take a seat," the woman at the desk told me.

"I don't think I can wait." I unfolded my arms to show her how the blood was seeping through the sleeves of my jumper, how my fingers were discoloured from all the blood that had trickled as I'd cut myself in that public toilet.

I felt sorry for the person who had to clean it. But not sorry enough to stick around. I had to get stitches, before I bled out. I'd already lost a lot of blood.

"Oh dear." Her eyes widened a fraction, then she schooled her expression. "Come with me."

I was hustled into the A&E, into a room, and then she disappeared. Presumably to get a doctor. I hoped anyway. My sleeves were absorbing the blood, but there were big patches of red and it was dripping down my wrists, over my hand, from my fingers. *Drip, drip, drip.*

"Oh my God." I bent over, fighting more tears, fighting the pain, fighting the faint feeling that over-came me. Fainting right now wouldn't do.

A man entered, middle-aged and definitely not Damian. *Isn't he at work today?* "Is Damian working? Doctor Fielding?"

The man took me in, curious. "You know him?" His eyebrows drew together in a frown, gaze resting on my face. We were so alike, Damian and I, we could've been brothers. And he must see it.

"Please, get a hold of him. I need—" I didn't know what I needed. I didn't want him to see me like this, but I also didn't want to be alone. "I need him or Josh or—" or Mathilda or Caesar or *anyone.* I just didn't want to be alone.

"I'll get someone to contact him for you." He left as quickly as he'd entered, but he came back almost immediately. His gaze now went directly to my arms. "You've done a number on yourself, lad." He sat down on a stool, wheeling over to me as he snapped on a pair of gloves.

I sat quietly as he very carefully tried to roll my sleeve up. "I think we have to be rid of the jumper completely." He stood now and motioned for me to lift my arms. I did, and he managed to peel the jumper off with minimal pain. Still, minimal pain meant that there was pain, and it hurt *a lot*.

Once it was thrown away in the rubbish—since clearly it wasn't anything to keep anymore, what with all the blood—he sat back down to inspect the damage.

I'd cut both my forearms in a frenzy and the result wasn't pretty. The result was bleeding profusely. The result was *horrible*.

He said something, but I didn't register what. It was like everything fell away. I couldn't hear anything. Couldn't see anything. I just closed my eyes and let him do as he saw fit. Let him do whatever he needed to do to stop the bleeding.

Time was non-existent. I sat there, eyes closed, feeling like my ears were stuffed with cotton. And it could've been one minute, or one hour, I didn't know. I didn't know anything at all.

I FELT WEAK, heavy, but I managed to blink my eyes open, though the lights were so bright, I had to squeeze them shut again in pain.

"Matt?"

That voice was familiar.

I inched my eyes open slowly and met Josh's worried, green eyes. "Josh." And just like that, everything came flooding back in. Caesar, the cutting, A&E… and I knew I must still be there, as I couldn't remember leaving. Last thing I could remember was that middle-aged doctor inspecting my arms. "Josh, I need help." My voice shook. "I need professional help."

The tears fell, my arms burned, my body felt too heavy to even move my head. My mind was a mess. One big, jumbled mess, swirling around and around and around. Everything was too much, bleak and dark and pitiful.

"I don't know what to do." I wanted to cover my face, for him not to see me cry like this, but I couldn't muster the energy to lift them.

"About what?" He leaned against the side of the bed or the trolley or whatever it was I was lying on, staring down at me.

"Everything!" It came out choked. "I don't— I'm more upset now about Caesar than I was when Dad *died*. There's something wrong with me. I've only known him for *days*." It shouldn't be possible to be so upset over someone you'd known less than a week. Or was it an actual week today? I'd lost count over the days too. "It's so messed up. I can't grieve for my dad, but I can for *him*. Something's very wrong with me."

"Nothing's wrong with you!" That was Mathilda, who was suddenly at my other side. "Matt…"

What was she doing here? Why had Josh brought her with him? And where was Damian? Was he there too? I couldn't find the strength to lift my head to check.

"We'll get you help, Matt." Josh squeezed my shoulder. "I'll call Vincent."

"No. I want someone I don't know, someone I will never meet outside of therapy." Josh's psychiatrist was something of a family friend, being the brother of Damian's best mate and all. The fact that Josh had been seeing him for the past decade probably had something to do with it too.

I didn't want to see someone who already knew all about me from Josh, or who knew everyone else around me. Finding someone who didn't know anyone I knew shouldn't be too hard, considering we lived in *London*.

"Okay." Josh nodded. "We'll find someone else.

I'm sure Vincent's got a lot of people to recommend. If that's okay with you?"

As long as I didn't have to talk to him. "Yeah. That's— that's okay." I didn't know what I could possibly say to a therapist, how to explain how I was feeling when I didn't even know myself, but they were there to help and I needed it. I needed help. I needed my head sorted out.

Josh smiled tightly. "You'll get through this."

He'd been struggling since he was a lot younger than me. For his whole bloody life, he'd been struggling. He'd been in therapy since he was sixteen. That was a long time. Was that the kind of timeframe I was looking at too? Certainly not. I'd never been abused, emotionally or sexually, but I did have issues. I knew they'd take time, that these kinds of things didn't just go away by themselves. Josh was proof of that. It wouldn't miraculously go away.

"What happened? Why am I lying down?" I must've fainted. *Oh my God.* Shame flooded through me.

"You lost consciousness." That was Damian's voice. He wasn't in my line of sight though, so I had no idea where he was actually standing. "They've given you an IV drip to get some fluid back into you. You lost a lot of blood."

Blood. My arms. "Has it stopped?"

"You've been stitched up quite nicely." Josh gave another of those tight smiles. We both had stitches now then.

"Why, Matt?" Mathilda's eyes brimmed with tears. "Why would you do this? Did you try to—to—"

"No." I hadn't tried to kill myself. I didn't want to *die*. Not really. I just needed to be in control, to feel something, to dull the bad feelings. "No. I would never do that."

"Really? You absolutely *sure* about that?" Her voice rose into a shrill. "Because your arms tell quite a different story!" She slapped her hands over her face as she turned away.

I finally managed to lift my head so I could look down on myself. The deepest cuts had been stitched shut, all the bleeding had stopped, and all the blood had been washed off. "Help me up." I felt dizzy as I struggled on my own, but managed it with Josh's help. I threw my feet over the edge, but I wasn't about to attempt standing just yet.

"Oh, Matt." Josh's hand hovered over my left forearm. I followed his gaze and saw what I'd carved into my skin. A heart line going down the entire underside. Spiking up and down, exactly like I remembered seeing on the machine as Caesar's heart threatened to give out.

I held my breath for a few heartbeats. "I messed up."

Josh's green gaze lifted to meet my eyes.

"I ran away." I was getting choked up again. "I just—I saw him, lying there, and I—I don't know. I just ran. He must hate me now."

"Apologise to him. I'm sure he'll understand." Josh's voice was soft, not berating or judging me in any kind of way.

"But *I* don't understand." We'd only known each other a week. How could he possibly want to deal with everything I had going for me? Or not going, as it were. I was a mess. He had epilepsy, yes, but he was a normal-functioning human being whereas I was neither normal nor functioning.

"I know it's difficult right now, but it gets better eventually." I heard Josh say it, but I didn't believe for a second that he believed it. Why would he be sporting his own stitches, after being harm-free for months, if it got better eventually?

"I'm such a bad person." I squeezed my eyes shut. I didn't want to see the stitches, the heart line, or the IV taped onto the back of my hand. I didn't want to see Josh either. I knew he was trying, but the bandages around his arms proved he wasn't doing much better himself. "I freak out when it's Caesar, but not when it's Dad."

"Remember what I told you last night? Shock. You've been in shock, Matt. And Ray... He was already gone by the time you were told, whereas with Caesar it happened right in front of you. No one witnessing something like that would've taken it calmly."

I opened my eyes again, but only stared down at my lap. I was wearing Adam's joggers, but they were stained with blood. *Oh no.* What had I done to myself? And now they were all here to see it... It didn't matter that Damian knew about my cutting, or that Josh had already known, but kept my secret because it hadn't been so bad back when he found out about it. Now they saw just how bad it was with their own eyes, and it was humiliating.

And Mathilda... I chanced a glance over my shoulder. She was standing close to the bed, looking down at my hand. Damian was at her side, but he was watching the almost-empty IV bag.

Mathilda was still on the verge of crying—and that got to me the most. I hadn't seen her cry since Dad died. She'd lost it that day, breaking down completely, and she'd been inconsolable for the next few days, all through the funeral. But once she got over it, she'd been so strong, never once falling back into the all-consuming grief. Whereas I—*I need to get my head on straight.* I was still a mess. Still trapped in the abyss.

"I want to go home." I wanted my bed, I wanted my journal, I wanted to be surrounded by *my* things. Not the sterile hospital, it only made me feel so much worse.

"Where's your jumper?" Josh looked around, as if he expected to see it folded neatly somewhere.

"Thrown away. It was full of blood." *Shit.* That meant I only had my T-shirt. That I'd have to walk out of A&E with my arms bare, the cuts and the stitches visible for all to see. "Oh no." I couldn't do that. I couldn't let anyone else see that, no matter if they were strangers or not. I *couldn't.*

A heavy weight settled on my shoulders, breaking me out of my panic. It was Damian's jacket, which he now settled firmly in place over my shoulders so it wouldn't fall down. I grabbed at the sides of it, drawing it close around me. Damian was both bigger and wider than me—I was thin and lanky, more like Josh in that sense—and the jacket pooled around me. It was warm from him having worn it and it was *good.*

"Thanks."

"Let's get you home." Damian's hand rested in-between my shoulder blades for a moment, then he stepped around the bed to stand at Josh's side. "Let me take the IV out, then we'll leave."

I nodded, eager for the whole hospital stay to be over and done with.

~

I DIDN'T KNOW how long I'd been lying curled up on my bed by the time my phone buzzed, but it must've been at least a couple of hours. I could only muster enough energy to reach out for the phone, then brought it back into the cocoon I'd made out of my duvet.

I didn't want to talk to anyone, but a certain spark of hope started in the pit of my stomach. My heart skipped a beat as I saw Caesar's name, my chest tightening in dread at what he had to say to me.

My finger hovered over the screen before I gathered my courage and slid the bar to unlock it.

Caesar: I'm sorry.

Just like that, my tears were back. For someone who hadn't cried once in years, I'd certainly cried a lot after meeting Caesar. Tears trickled down my cheeks to wet my pillow.

Me: You've got nothing to be sorry for.

I had to start the text over three times because my fingers kept hitting the wrong letters on the touch-screen keyboard.

Caesar: I should've told u. But I was afraid.

I sniffled as I read those words. *Afraid*. Maybe he should've told me, but we'd only known each other a week, so I understood why he hadn't. It was a private matter and we didn't know each other *that* well. We'd just had awesome, incredible sex, but hardly any heart-to-hearts. It wasn't like I'd voluntarily told him about my cutting, either.

Me: What were you afraid of?

Caesar was bold and brash and unafraid. What could he possibly have to fear?

Caesar: That u'd leave me.

The words hit me hard and I gasped through a loud sob escaping me. My thumbs trembled as I tried to write a reply.

Me: I'm so sorry, Caesar!

I hadn't meant to run away. I'd wanted to go into that room and make sure he was okay. I'd wanted to touch him, to feel that his body was warm and breathing and alive. I'd wanted to kiss him and hug him and never bloody let him go again.

Instead I'd run off like a coward. I'd been unable to face it. Unable to face him, who had been nothing but kind to me. Who had let me stay with him for an entire weekend, because I didn't want to go home. Also for the sex, obviously.

Caesar: It's ok, Matty. I understand. I wouldn't want 2 be around some1 with my condition either.

I squeezed my eyes shut after reading that reply. How could he *understand*? How could he play it off so casually? I *did* want to be around him. What I *didn't* want was to let him go.

Me: We were good together, don't you think?

We *had* been. I'd felt better with Caesar around the past week than I had in three years. With him I could relax, I could enjoy myself, I could *laugh*.

Caesar had introduced me to pleasures I hadn't even known existed.

Caesar: Yeah… we were. I really liked what we had, Matty.

I cradled my phone to my chest as I worked out what to write next.

Me: Me too. I don't want it to end.

There it was, the absolute truth. If he felt like I did, he must've been miserable ever since I ran out of his hospital room, just as I'd been miserable for running away. I couldn't quite believe I'd turned into such a drama queen. And what had happened after… the visit to Adam, the cutting, A&E, the fainting… I was ashamed.

But to hell with sorting my head out. I just wanted Caesar. Even if he had grand mal seizures—or whatever new terminology Damian had called them—that could cause his heart to stop, I wanted him. I wanted what we'd had together the past week; I wanted us to have *more*.

Caesar: It doesn't have 2 end.

I stared at the words. *He still wants me!* Even after I'd acted like a twat, he still wanted me. My phone vibrated as another text popped in.

Caesar: Can I c u in a couple of days?

I frowned.

Me: Why a couple of days?

I wanted to see him *now*. I certainly didn't want to wait longer than tomorrow.

Caesar: I have 2 rest. The folks won't let me out of the house b4 they know I'm fine. I really want to c u, Matty.

Well, that made sense. His body had been through a lot, so I could understand he needed his rest. Maybe I'd even get myself a bit more sorted out before I saw him again. I didn't think I'd get to see any kind of professional that quickly though, but at least I could stay at home, relax, try to forget the roller coaster of emotions I'd gone through.

Matt: I'm looking forward to it.

I typed another sentence after that one was sent.

My finger hovered over the send button, but I chick-ened out and pressed the home button instead. I could see the small sentence clearly in my mind though as I let the phone fall onto the bed.

I think I'm in love with you. It might be soon, too soon everyone else would say, but I really thought I might be.

CHAPTER 16

I heard the door open and close, but I couldn't find the strength to care. Or to even move. What did it matter, anyway? Either it was Mathilda, who wanted to make sure I wasn't dead, or it was Josh who wanted to make sure I ate, or Damian who wanted to make sure I wasn't trying to kill myself. Or their roles could be reversed. What did I know? What did I care?

No one said anything. I could hear a faint rustle of clothes, of the floorboards creak under someone's weight. But they, whoever one of them it was, didn't say a single word.

I peeked out of my fort, my cocoon, and nearly lost my breath altogether. Because it wasn't Damian or Josh or Mathilda—it was Caesar.

He must've heard me, because his head turned towards the bed. "Jesus, Matty." He took a startled step back upon spotting me. "I thought you weren't home."

"Where else would I be?" I was where I belonged. Question was, what was he doing here?

His eyes were a bit bigger than usual as he stared at me. He was dressed like he used to though, almost exactly like he had the night I'd met him. *Today's one week. One week since we met. Feels like so much longer.* He looked amazing. He was fine and he was *alive* and he was *here*.

"What are *you* doing here?" Wasn't he supposed to be resting? He said himself yesterday that his parents wouldn't let him out of the house. Yet here he was.

"I wanted to see you." He rocked back on the soles of his feet, and he seemed… nervous.

"They let you out?" I pushed the duvet further down so my entire face was bared for him to see. My arms though— they were kept safely away from his eyes. He'd said he didn't mind, back when I only had the scars, but now, with the sutures… They weren't pretty. If I'd known I'd have visitors I never would've been lying here in a T-shirt.

"I'm a grown-up. They can't keep me in if I don't

want to stay there." He came closer, gazing down at me. "Besides, I feel a lot better today."

I stared back. "You've got a hell of a lot of explaining to do." It came out harsh, angry, when I really wasn't. I wasn't angry with him at all. If anything, I was happy he was here. I just wished I hadn't been such a mess.

"I know. I'm sorry." He glanced away, ashamed.

I wanted to hug him, but I couldn't sit up, because then my arms would be bared.

"Mum and Dad said you were there when—" He cleared his voice, unable to say what exactly had happened.

"Yeah."

"I'm so sorry, Matty." And he did sound upset and sincere about it.

"It's okay. As long as you're fine, it's okay." I clutched at the end of the duvet. "I told the paramedics I was your boyfriend, so they'd let me ride in the ambulance with you."

It brought a wry smile to his lips. "Did you, huh?"

I bit my lip, courage failing me. Then I told myself off for being such a coward—like I *always* had been, since I'd never told anyone anything—and decided it was time to change that. "I want to be your boyfriend."

Maybe he didn't feel the same way. Maybe for him it really was just sex, although I didn't think so, else he wouldn't be here right now. Although if it was and I'd taken a chance for nothing— well. Then maybe keeping my mouth shut about everything had been the right thing to do, after all.

"Really? You want that?" He blinked at me. "Even after what you saw? What happened? It can happen again, you know, I have no control over it—"

"Especially after that." I finally sat up, but clutched the duvet close against my chest so it wouldn't fall down and expose my arms. "I like being with you. I know it's only been a week, but— a relationship has to start somewhere, right? And I want it. I want the label, I want the exclusivity, I want it all with *you*."

His eyes had widened a fraction during my little speech, but once I finished he was smiling. Some of the cocky arrogance I knew was back in it too. "I want that too, Matty."

I smiled back, my chest squeezing, the butterflies going wild in my gut. "Want to make it official?"

"With a kiss?" He leaned forward and down.

I leaned up too to meet him, our lips sliding together. "A kiss is always nice. But I was thinking more of adding it on Facebook."

Caesar laughed as he flopped down on the bed.

"I'm hardly ever on there. And we're not even friends."

"Now *that* has to be rectified, doesn't it?" I wanted to do it now. But my mobile was on the bedside table and I had to reach out to get it. I couldn't get myself to do that. Our chat was going so well, but perhaps it wouldn't if he saw the evidence of what exactly I'd done to myself.

"Damian says alcohol triggers seizures." It was time to change the subject to something more serious. "You're never drinking again, okay, because I don't ever want to see them fight to keep your heart beating."

Caesar swallowed so heavily I heard it. "I have a reason to stay away from anything potentially dangerous now." He glanced at me, the meaning behind it clear.

It warmed me. It warmed my broken, lost heart a *lot*. But the meaning behind those words, they chilled me. "You mean you've been drinking on purpose? That you've wanted a seizure like that? A serious one?"

He ran a hand over the lower part of his face. "Self-destruction is a funny thing. I had nothing going for me. I've got no particular friends, only acquaintances. People don't tend to want anything more than a shag from me, but I guess that's my own fault, considering I *am* a bit of a slag. And a disorder that I can't ever escape… I guess I was thinking if I just lived life, partied hard, it would end sooner, you know?"

It was my turn to swallow a lump in my throat. "Maybe you should seek out a therapist too."

He met my gaze now. "You're seeing a therapist? I thought you said—"

"It's time." I cursed myself for having revealed that. But I suppose if I'd already said A, I had to say B too. It wasn't like I could sit under the duvet for his entire visit, after all. "I'm a wreck. I went too far. I cut myself too deep."

His lips parted, as if he wanted to say something, but then he just sat there. Maybe he wasn't sure what to say. Maybe he regretted being involved with me.

It took him a while, but he finally found his voice. "What do you mean you cut too deep? You—did you try to—?"

Something icy went through me. "No! No, I wouldn't—not *that!*" Why did everyone think I wanted to kill myself just because I cut myself? I *didn't*. I wanted to live—it was just hard and the cutting helped. "I cut so deep I needed sutures. But not over the main artery or anything like that." *Never that.*

I thrust my arms out for him to see. See the older

scars, the new cuts that weren't so deep they'd needed stitching, and the sutures themselves.

He drew in a sharp breath. "Mum and Dad said you had to be sedated. Did you do this before or after?"

"After. The day after. After I ran away from your room."

"Oh." He frowned.

I didn't want to talk about my cutting. "Why're you living alone if you have epilepsy? Couldn't that be dangerous?" Though, I suppose a lot of adult folk did have to live alone and deal with it.

"That's why I've got my dog. She's a seizure response dog." He smiled affectionately at the mention of his dog. I, belatedly, realised I didn't know her name—and that I'd never asked. "And besides, I haven't actually had a bad one like that in years. Usually I just sleep it off."

The front door banged, startling me, as I'd been so intent on him and what he was saying.

"Joshua!"

"What's Angie doing here?" And slamming doors, nonetheless. Caesar only shrugged, but then he didn't know who that was. "She's Josh's mother."

"Oh, the blond, yeah. He was kind of… strange earlier." Caesar gave an apologetic smile.

"He's borderline," I said, hoping it would explain,

but Caesar only looked at me blankly. On the other side of my door I heard Angelina's heels click over the floor. "Emotionally unstable."

I stood from the bed and padded over to the door, opening enough to peek out. "Hey. What's going on?"

"Where's Josh?" She came out from the kitchen and strode over to Josh and Damian's bedroom door. "Is Damian at work?"

"Yeah." Or I suppose he was, anyway, considering he hadn't come investigating the slamming of doors.

She went into the room, not caring about their privacy, but quickly came back out. Her face was the epitome of worry. "Has Josh been home? Has he gone out?"

"He's home. I don't think he's gone out again." I gripped the door tight, a bad feeling overtaking me as Angelina's gaze settled on the bathroom door.

"Joshua?" She strode over, hand on the handle. When there was no answer, she pressed it down. The door opened, to both our relief, it seemed—then stopped, as if it met resistance. "Joshua?"

Oh no. I knew something was wrong. Angelina knew it too, I could tell from the expression on her face.

"Joshua?" She pressed on the door some more,

but it didn't move. There was no sound from inside the bathroom. "Joshua!" She put her whole weight against the door—and it finally inched open some more.

I couldn't move. I was frozen to the floor. *Not again*. Not someone else. Not *Josh*.

"Matt, ring Damian!" She'd gone into the room, so I couldn't see her anymore.

"But—what about an ambulance?"

"I'm ringing now, just get a hold of Damian so he's prepared, so he can meet us at A&E!" She greeted someone else, voice not so loud anymore.

"Matty?" Caesar's hands touched my shoulder, startling me, bringing me into action. "You have to do what she says. You have to ring him."

I couldn't. I couldn't ring Damian and tell him that his boyfriend was—what? Was he unconscious? Was he bleeding out? Was he *dead*? What had Josh done? *Why* had he done it? He'd been doing so well!

I dived for my phone, but once I had it in my hand I froze up again. I turned my head to look at Caesar, who was standing quietly besides me. "You have to go help her. She'll need help."

He nodded, but hesitated slightly. "You ring him, okay?"

"I will." I nodded jerkily. "I *am*." Caesar left me alone and I unlocked the mobile screen and went into my recent contacts. Damian's name was there and my thumb hovered over it. *What am I going to say? How am I going to say it?*

Your boyfriend tried to kill himself. He might've succeeded. That was the truth, but I couldn't say it like that. But how else could I phrase it?

I pressed down on his name, stared as it started ringing, then fumbled the phone up to my ear as Damian answered immediately. "Matt?"

My breath hitched. This was it. He was on the other end. I had to say something. I had to tell him. "Damian…"

I couldn't do it. I couldn't tell him. But I had to. So I took a deep breath—and then I told him.

CHAPTER 17

*D*amian was standing outside the hospital once we arrived in Angelina's car.

He was leaning against the wall, head tilted up, eyes closed. My chest squeezed so tight I almost wasn't able to breathe—because why would Damian be outside when Josh was *inside*?

Why wasn't he at Josh's side?

"Oh no, no, no." Angelina was out of the car before I even managed to unbuckle.

I cast a glance at Caesar, whose expression I couldn't read, then I was out and heading after her. *Josh can't be— can he?* Fear squeezed my chest tighter, so I literally had to fight to take a breath.

"Why are you out *here*?" Angelina stopped in front of Damian, who opened his eyes to focus on her. "Josh? Is he—*Please*. No." She shook her head, eyes wide and terrified.

"He's not—" Damian's voice gave out on him, and this was the most shook up I'd ever seen him. Besides three years ago, obviously, when Josh's life had again been hanging in a small thread. "He woke up. He was hallucinating. About Andrew. About *that* day." I could see his throat working as he swallowed heavily several times.

There could only be the one *that day*. The day Andrew, who'd been released from prison, had attacked Josh in our house, slamming his head against our kitchen table. Then he'd gone on to kill my dad. Accident or not, he was the one responsible.

Caesar's hands briefly squeezed my shoulders to let me know he was there behind me. I was glad he'd come with us. Josh was Angelina's son, Damian's significant other, and they had enough to deal with themselves. If I fell apart, Caesar would be there to pull me back up again.

Damian's eyes flickered, he looked like he wanted to say something else, but then he simply turned and strode back into the hospital. Angelina was close on his heels, but I couldn't move. I couldn't go in there. Last time I'd been in the hospital, I'd run away. The time before I'd been so hysterical I'd had to be sedated. And the time before then my dad had been *dead* and Josh had nearly died. What if he died this time?

"Hey…" Caesar's arms slid around my shoulder, and his warm, steady body showed me just how cold I was and how much I was trembling.

"I'm scared." There was so much in that word. Scared of going inside, of what would meet me inside, of Josh dying, of anyone dying, of my own mental health. Was I going to be the next one admitted to hospital for a suicide attempt? One I meant to do or not? What if next time I cut too deep and there was no one there to help me?

"Yeah." Caesar rested his cheek against my temple, not saying anything else. I was glad he didn't make me any promises, because no matter what promises could be made, one could never be sure they'd actually be upheld. Neither he, nor I, knew if Josh would die or not.

A sob escaped me. "God, no."

"Hey, shhh." He rocked us gently. "Don't think about the worst-case scenario."

"How can I not? He did that on *purpose*." My throat was closing up. It was difficult to speak, to even *breathe*. "He's done it many times. What are the odds of surviving all of them?"

"Let's go inside. Let's wait and see. They're helping him in there. That's what they're here for."

Caesar pushed me gently, causing me to take a couple steps, bringing us closer to the double doors.

I knew that. Of course I did. But they hadn't been able to help my dad. They *had* been able to help Caesar. They'd helped me… stitched me up when I needed it. Damian had sedated me when I needed it. That was a lot of help, but what if it was time to let someone die, time for them not to be able to help?

Not Josh. No, he can't die.

I couldn't lose anyone else. *Damian* couldn't lose anyone else. Josh was his *life*. They'd been together for so long. It wasn't fair that this happened now. Why had Josh done something so drastic? There might not even be a proper reason, I knew that, what with Josh being emotionally unstable, but… *how* could he do it now? He had a good life. Couldn't he just forget about that bastard of an ex-stepfather and be happy with Damian? With us? He had been doing so well…

He couldn't leave us. He just couldn't.

What were we going to do without him? What was *I* going to do if I lost anyone else? I couldn't lose anyone else. I couldn't take it.

JOSH WAS OUT OF DANGER, though the doctors couldn't

say if he'd ever be himself again. He was still suffering side effects from the pills he'd swallowed, but at least he was *alive*.

I wasn't allowed in to see him, no one were really, though Angelina popped in for a quick check. Damian, on the other hand, sat at his side, and he wasn't planning on leaving.

So Angelina drove Caesar and me back to the flat, where she followed us inside. When she headed towards Josh and Damian's bedroom, I followed hesitantly. "What are you doing?"

"Joshua's going to need clothes. He'll also want his journal, his mobile, and perhaps his laptop." If he'd even be lucid enough to do that. If the overdose hadn't ruined something inside him, hadn't damaged him for life.

I didn't say it though. I could tell she was thinking it.

She scooped joggers and jumpers into a bag she drew from the closet. Damian must've told her where things were, because I couldn't image she'd know such things otherwise.

"Josh has an appointment with Vincent Monday morning." She said it matter-of-factly, then looked up at me. "You're going to take that one."

"Wha—no! I don't want to go see Vincent." I took a step back from the force of her gaze and her words.

"You're taking it, Matthew. Neither Damian nor I, nor Joshua, wants the next time to be you. Considering the state of your arms, it will be."

I crossed my arms self-consciously, even though I was wearing a zipped jumper now that hid them well. No one could tell I had god-knew-how-many stitches in my skin.

She had a point though. I didn't want to feel so bad I voluntarily swallowed tablets or cut my arms up from wrist to elbow. I didn't want any of them to have to find me, to worry about me, to try and keep me alive, to grieve for me if I died. I didn't want to die. I did want to live, of course I did. It was just hard. Everything was so *hard*.

"I'll come pick you up Monday morning." She stood, the bag was all zipped, and she now hoisted it up on one shoulder. She grabbed the laptop from the desk, and the journal next to it, then swept past me. "I'll be back later with dinner. Until then— don't worry, Matt. Take care of yourself. And don't do anything stupid." Her gaze bore into me at the last part and I nodded mutely.

Once she was gone, Caesar stepped up to me. "Do you want me to stay? I can go home. I'll understand if you want to be alone."

I drew a shaky breath. "I don't think being alone is such a good thing for me right now." *Honesty*. Josh was always all about honesty, on speaking your feelings. He hadn't today and look what that had led to. I didn't want to end up like that.

He nodded, solemn. "I'll stay then."

"I wonder where Mathilda is." I gazed towards her closed bedroom door. She wasn't home, or else she would've been out to investigate long before now. Back when Angelina had been banging into the flat and shouting for Josh, or now when we'd all come back. "She doesn't know yet."

"You can ring her," Caesar suggested, "or just wait for her to come home."

I didn't know what would be the right thing. I didn't want to ring her, because she might panic. She might think along the lines of our dad, that we'd lost someone else… but waiting for her—I didn't even know what she was up to. What I would be interrupting. How far away she was.

"Come on." Caesar grabbed my shoulders and steered me over to the sofa, where he pushed me down. "I'd suggest you have a nap, because you're clearly not doing okay, but I'm guessing that's not something you're going to be able to do."

I shook my head. "Too much to think about."

He sat down next to me, a hard, warm body for me to lean against. And I did—I tipped over to rest my head on his shoulder. "I bet you regret getting with me now."

"Why would you think that?" He sounded nonplussed.

"Because of all of this. My issues— Josh attempting suicide."

His chest rose in a deep breath. "He was acting weird when he let me in. I noticed it—and I just left him in the kitchen to go wait for you. I never should've done that."

I tensed. *He's blaming himself?* "No, Caesar. Just— no. This isn't your fault. Josh is always a bit... odd. It comes with the diagnosis. He's borderline. Emotionally unstable." Maybe that's what I was too. It sure seemed like it. "He's tried it before, you know. Suicide. It's also part of the diagnosis. Suicide is a lot more likely in people with BPD than people who're not borderline. I don't remember the percentage, but it's a high one."

"That seems like an awfully scary thing to live with. I'd worry all the time."

I stiffened, words on the tips of my tongue that if he wanted to stay with me, maybe he'd have to keep on worrying— but the front door opening drew my attention.

Mathilda greeted us with a smile. "How're you feeling, Matt?" She took Caesar in, mouth quirking a bit more. She was humoured by the fact he was here —maybe she'd expected him to be, maybe she was just happy that he made *me* happy.

But I wasn't happy. Not now. "Mathilda."

She stopped smiling once she focused back on me. "What's wrong?" Her hands clenched at her sides and I could see fear fill her. She must've seen it on my face, seen something... I didn't know how my face looked, but it sure didn't look anywhere close to cheerful or happy.

"It's Josh. He's in hospital." I gripped Caesar's upper arm as I watched her blink, digesting the words. "He swallowed tablets. He tried to—"

"*Why?*"

"I don't know." Who could know what went on in Josh's mind at all times? "Maybe it was just an impulse..." That also came with the diagnosis.

She dropped down heavily on the sofa. "Tell me everything that happened."

So I did.

CHAPTER 18

A fleeting feeling
happiness
Quickly replaced
dark and bleak
No more elation
Utter
desolation

This was it.

The door loomed in front of me. I didn't want to be there, I wanted to turn around and go back home. Go back to bed, bury myself under the covers. That was safe, that was… unhealthy. I knew it, rationally, but it still didn't mean I wanted to be there.

It opened.

"Hi, Matthew." Vincent smiled at me, holding it open for me to brush past him inside.

I think I muttered a greeting in return, but my mind was so heavy, so far away I couldn't be sure. I perched in one of the comfy chairs set up. We were facing each other, with a table between us. I rocked back and forth, unsure and uncertain and so goddamn *tired*.

He sat down across from me, gaze levelled on me, taking me in, sizing me up.

It was unnerving. "Josh is in hospital," I blurted out. I wasn't sure he knew, but then he must've, because he'd greeted me like it wasn't a surprise to see me here instead of Josh. Angelina must've rung him.

"I know. I've been to see him."

I lifted my head at that. "You were allowed to?" I hadn't been allowed to see him yet. Damian had stayed at the hospital at Josh's side all weekend, but neither Mathilda nor I had been allowed to be there. Josh wasn't back to himself yet, though Angelina had been hopeful yesterday when she'd been over with dinner for us.

"I'm his psychologist." Vincent nodded briefly. "How do you feel?"

How did I feel? It was all a mess. "Like a mess.

Heavy, tired, like nothing matters." I swallowed. "Lost." That summed it up nicely.

He nodded again, thoughtful. "Everything that's said in here is confidential. You know that, right?"

"Yeah."

"I can only break confidentiality if I feel you're a danger to yourself and others. You understand that?"

"I don't want to die." That must be what he was getting at. I wasn't a danger to anyone but myself, after all. "I just don't want to live." It wasn't the same thing. I didn't actively want to kill myself—it was just that living was *hard*. I wished, without wanting to do anything about it myself, that I didn't have to anymore.

He lowered his eyes to the notebook resting on one knee, and he wrote something in it. Probably suicidal, even if I wasn't. It sounded like it, didn't it?

"I want to get a diagnosis on you, Matthew." He still wrote as he said it.

Diagnosis? "Yeah."

"But it takes time. There's questionnaires and interview-like sessions required. Standard questions required for you to answer, so that I can get a good grasp on you and your psyche. And from there, a good pinpoint on a correct diagnosis." His pencil scratched against the paper. "It'll take three to four sessions to finish that, then I'll get together with my team, and we'll go through it, finding the diagnosis. I don't want to start you on any medicine before we've got a diagnosis down on paper."

"Why not?" I wanted medicine. I *needed* it to function. "Can't you just give me antidepressants?" Those were supposed to make the depression go away, make me feel alive and happy again.

He shook his head sadly. "I'm afraid not, Matthew. If, for example, your diagnosis turns out to be bipolar, antidepressants are very likely to make it worse."

"Bipolar?" Manic-depression. "I'm not." That was highs and lows and hallucinations—at least Josh's friend had it like that—and I didn't. I didn't have highs and I definitely didn't have hallucinations.

"That's what we'll figure out."

I drew in a shaky breath, something heavy settling over me again. No medicine. Nothing to make me feel better. "Can it be figured out quickly?"

"We'll figure it out, Matthew. Don't worry. We'll get there."

I didn't believe him. How could I? Josh had been in therapy for so many years, and now he was back exactly where he started. But he *had* been doing better. He always did better. Until he didn't. "Do you think Josh will get better again?" If Josh couldn't get better, what chance did I have?

"I do. Josh is strong. I think you're strong too."

I didn't believe that either. I didn't think I was strong at all. Maybe I'd used to be—but I couldn't remember a time where I'd thought so about myself. Not a single time.

~

I KNOCKED on the door and stood back to wait.

I heard barking from inside, so if the dog was home, I hoped Caesar would be as well. Considering how he'd been going on about not wanting her to be alone.

The door did open and a moist, cold snout pushed against my hand. I smiled down at the dog, scratching her behind the ear. I really should ask her name. I still didn't know it.

Seeing her though, it brought back memories I didn't want to think about. Memories of *my* dog. My parents had got her for me just before Dad died. She was dead now, just like him. I hadn't cried for her either. I shut it all out. All of it. I couldn't deal.

I lifted my head to look at Caesar, and found him gazing at me in a certain kind of way… a way that made all my blood head south.

"Hey, Matty." He held the door open wider, inviting me in.

He looked so good. His hair a mess, like he'd just got out of bed, and those stylish glasses perched on his nose. He was only wearing a vest—a loose one, so I could see his nipples peaking out.

He licked his lips. My eyes followed the movement.

My cock was interested. It hadn't been at all interested in anything during the weekend, or the days before it, but now it definitely was. It pressed against my tight, skinny jeans.

It'd only been one day since I'd last seen him. He'd stayed with me Friday night, left Saturday afternoon to visit his parents. Sunday he hadn't been around, I'd been alone. I'd liked it, being on my own, buried under my duvet. But now... seeing him standing there with ruffled hair and his upper chest on display... I realised just how much I'd missed him.

"Matty?" His expression, which had been happy to see me, now turned uncertain.

I'd likely be ashamed of it later, but right there and then it didn't matter. I simply threw myself at him, wrapped my arms around his shoulders and connected my lips with his.

He didn't even hesitate about reciprocating. It turned from my originally chaste but hard kiss, to one more desperate, passionate.

We moved into the flat, and Caesar shut the door once he heard the dog's claws click on the floor. We moved over the floor, towards the bedroom, where I pushed him down on the bed and climbed on top of him. It felt so good to kiss him.

He's my boyfriend. I'd never had one of those before. I'd never given relationships much thought— not even with Adam, considering he'd always been in one. As long as I'd known him, at least. I hadn't thought Caesar would turn out to be my boyfriend either, not after just that one night. Life was strange sometimes though. Strange and difficult and sad and sometimes even *good*.

He brought his tongue out to play and my limbs turned to jelly. His tongue did such wonderful things to me; I was pretty sure I moaned—loud.

His hands travelled up my side, over my shoulders and down my back until they cupped my arse. He squeezed and I bucked against him, already leaking from anticipation.

A hand slipped down the front of my jeans and made quick work of the buttons. The flaps were pulled apart and the jeans inched down over my hips a little until my cock slipped free from its confinement.

I definitely moaned when one of his warm hands wrapped around my dick. It'd been too long since I'd had his hands on me—at least in this way. I was hooked on Caesar's touch after only a week with him. He was *that* addictive.

He kept just the right amount of tightness as he stroked me. I continued to leak, adding some natural slick to the friction.

I ground my arse down against his groin, and I could feel his own hard cock trapped inside his loose joggers. I reached down with one hand, bypassing his around my own dick, to slip it under his waistband, wrapping it around a hard shaft.

He shoved at my chest with his free hand and I willingly let myself tilt to the side, falling down onto my back at his side. He pushed up to hover over me, his hand still stroking me.

I gazed up at him through half-lidded eyes. "Are you up to this?" I didn't want him to participate in something that could send him right back into another seizure. Though sex... was that really a seizure-inducing activity? I still spread my legs so he could lower himself between them, hooking them around his waist.

"Of course. I've been resting for *days*." Our chests lined up as he trailed nibbling kisses down my throat.

I tilted my head back and to the side, giving him all the space he needed. I moaned, my hand tightening around his dick as I stroked it in the exact same, lazy rhythm he was stroking me.

I tangled my other hand in his hair, loving the feel of the thick, dark strands sliding against the thin, ticklish skin of my fingertips and palm.

"God, you feel good." It came out on a groan.

"You too." My grip on his hair tightened as his hand sped up on my cock. "You make me feel so good." No one made me feel as good as Caesar did.

"It's because I have my hand on your dick." He chuckled, then licked his way up my neck before delivering a soft kiss to my lips.

"Obviously. But—You *always* make me feel good. Not just in bed, though the sex is amazing, I got to give you that."

A pleased grin spread over his lips before he ducked his head to my neck again. He sucked on the skin he'd just licked and I let out another loud moan at the thrills shooting through my body.

My hand on him faltered as my orgasm started to rise. I clung tightly as I came with a low cry, hips bucking frantically. He stroked me through it, until I was entirely spent and starting to soften. Once I was lying there in post-orgasmic bliss, completely numb and unable to move, he lifted himself up so he could look down at me. He smiled wryly, his hand coming up, offered to my lips. I opened and licked the semen that clung to his skin off. *My semen.*

"Want to suck me off?" His voice had gone low, husky.

"Oh yeah." I watched his cock bounce as he moved to position himself perfectly for a blowjob. His knees rested on both sides of my chest, right up under my armpits.

I gazed up at him, seeing the lust mirrored in his eyes, then lifted my head to reach the rigid shaft. I licked a line up the underside, from root up to the plump head. I was in no mood to tease though—I wanted this to happen, and I wanted it to happen *now.* I opened my mouth and sucked him in.

With a groan, Caesar moved his hips experimentally. I held onto his hips as I bobbed my head with his movements. He seemed to be in a hurry to get off too because the speed quickened fast. I didn't mind.

I could tell he was close from the way he bit his lower lip and how his hips faltered. I debated pulling away, letting him come over my face—there was something erotic about that—but I decided against it. I wanted to taste him, to swallow it. So I did. I swallowed what he had to give and then licked him clean before I pulled off and let my head fall back down onto the rumpled sheets.

He fell sideways onto the bed with a *huff,* running

his fingers through his hair before he turned to me. "You're amazing." He caressed my face, thumb particularly fond of my lips. "You're so fucking amazing, Matty."

I would rather say so about Caesar, but it was nice to hear nonetheless. I settled for a simple smile and rolled over onto my side to be closer to him.

"I never thought it would turn out like this that night," he whispered. "You looked so sad and lost, sitting there, and I thought I'd simply offer you a drink."

"Why didn't you think it'd turn into this?" I hadn't either, but I wasn't about to share that. Instead I let my gaze roam his face, taking in everything about him that I could see. The smooth skin, with a hint of stubble, the straight nose, the high cheek-bones, the thin yet kissable lips, the warm green eyes framed by thick, black eyelashes… The glasses were gone. I had no idea when or where he'd discarded them, but he looked just as hot without them, so I didn't mind.

"Things don't ever really work out for me rela-tionship-wise." There was resignation to his voice. "Usually people I've been interested in couldn't deal with my epilepsy and the one person who could, well, he couldn't deal with my personality."

"Personality?" I frowned. There was nothing at all

wrong about Caesar's personality. In fact, it was that which kept me from succumbing into that big, black hole right this moment. Caesar was happy and smiling and good to be around—perfect after a hard session of bearing my feelings to Josh's psychologist.

"I'm too out there, you know. Too flamboyant. Too *gay*." I could tell that it was the last brush-off that was hardest for him to stomach. Not because of the reason—I suspected Caesar liked being instantly pegged as gay. He wore his sexuality on his sleeve, as it were—but because the person who had brushed him off had been important to him.

"That was Alistair, wasn't it?" I remembered him telling me they'd used to be mates. Clearly something had happened to make that past tense.

"Yeah. We were mates, you know. He never laughed or teased whenever I had a seizure at school. I guess maybe I misinterpreted him. I thought he fancied me as more than a mate, but I was wrong. He doesn't want to be gay so he doesn't want someone who looks gay."

"*Is* he gay?" My eyebrows scrunched together in a frown. Mathilda had never mentioned any of her mates being gay—but then that wasn't exactly a normal topic of conversation, was it? Nick, I knew was gay, but only because he was in a relationship with Adam.

"Closet case. Or bi. I don't know." His hand came back to caress my cheek, then it slid upwards into my hair. "Plus he's got homophobic parents. He almost never brought me round to his place back when we were mates. I've always been too obvious, you know?"

"I think you're just perfect." I might've hidden myself in a closet too, but now I'd met someone, I hadn't been afraid to come out. I couldn't rationally explain why I'd even been afraid of coming out before, it was just— it didn't make any sort of sense. But then when had my head ever made much sense?

"Sweet talker." He bent over to kiss me, but the smile he couldn't stop told me loud and clear he was pleased with my words. I liked seeing him pleased, it pleased me even more. "So what now?"

"Hmm?" I stared up into his eyes. They seemed to be shining, alongside his big smile. *He's happy. And it's because of me.* The realisation knocked me breathless.

How could *I*, miserable person that I was, make someone so happy? I couldn't be in charge of anyone else's happiness when my own was non-existent.

"Will you stay for a bit?"

"A little bit. But I have to go home soon. Mathilda's there all alone." My throat closed up at the thought of Josh in hospital... but out of immediate danger.

He sobered. "How did your first therapy session go?"

"Not as bad as expected." I'd expected it all to go to hell. I *knew* Vincent—well, knew *of* him, anyway—but it hadn't been as awkward and difficult to speak as I'd imagined.

I didn't want to think about therapy though. I didn't want to think about Mathilda, all alone at home because Josh had been admitted to hospital and Damian there too, because he wasn't going to leave Josh's side.

I threw my leg over his waist and rubbed my cock up against his clothed stomach. "I'm hard again. I really think you should do something about that."

He laughed out loud, eyes twinkling as he looked at me. Then he shimmied down my torso and did exactly what I'd asked of him.

CHAPTER 19

I came home to find Adam in my living room.

The minute he saw me slump through the front door, he strode up to me and gathered me up in a tight hug. His arms, muscular and strong, were like a vice around me and it felt like I simply melted against him. *This feels good.*

"I'm so sorry. I heard what happened."

He cupped the back of my neck, keeping me there close to him. He smelled of aftershave and cologne and his body was warm and hard and fit.

I wasn't quite sure what he was referring to though. So much had happened. It was probably Josh. Surely he couldn't know about Caesar or what

I'd done to myself? I hadn't told him when I'd been over there—

Shame washed over me at the thought of my last visit to Adam. I'd been a complete mess. I never should've gone to him in the first place. I shouldn't be having a crush on him, either, considering he was already taken. Had been since I'd even got to know him.

And also... I'd told Caesar I wanted the whole thing with him; relationship, exclusivity. I couldn't go around having a crush on someone else after having asked that of *him*.

I felt ashamed all over again.

Adam let me go, or at least held me at an arm's length as he looked me over. "Hate to tell you, mate, but you look like shit."

"Yeah." I managed a tight smile. I felt like shit too. The outside did tend to mirror the inside with me.

"It's going to be okay." He briefly cupped my cheek, then gave me a thump on the shoulder. "Come on, Les's making dinner."

"Wha—Leslie's here?" Now that he mentioned it, I could hear sounds coming from the kitchen.

I followed him into the brightly lit room, and found both Mathilda and Leslie sitting at the table, chatting amiably. Something was bubbling in the oven. It smelled heavenly.

"Hi, Matt." Leslie smiled at me.

"Hi." I glanced between him and Adam, unsure what they were doing here. Had Angelina asked them over? Or had Damian? Josh couldn't have, since he wasn't aware enough to do anything at the moment.

"I thought you both could use a proper, home-cooked meal." Leslie rose to check the timer on the counter, then he opened the oven door and put four baguettes in. "Lasagna and garlic bread."

"It sounds like heaven. It *smells* like heaven." Mathilda turned to grin at me.

I didn't understand how she could look so happy —but she was stronger than me, and she didn't suffer from depression. If indeed that was what was wrong with me, and not something more complex. Not that depression wasn't complex, but— I hoped I wasn't bipolar. Or even borderline, like Josh, but I didn't think that was the case. I was just... depressed. That was all.

The table was already decked—for four. I took my place opposite Mathilda, and Adam sat down next to me. It wasn't the biggest table, so our knees kept brushing as we both moved around to find comfort-able positions.

It wasn't quite the same anymore though, touching him. I had Caesar—and I liked what we'd begun. I wanted to keep on exploring, keep on being with him, see where we'd end up. There was no guarantee we'd end up with a happily ever after—like Damian and Josh, they'd found each other when they were both eighteen and they were still together—but for now I wanted what we had.

Even if Adam had, by some miraculous way, been available and interested… I thought I'd rather have stayed with Caesar. Adam was a good mate, and I couldn't help the flicker of attraction I still felt towards him, because he really was a handsome lad, but so was Caesar. And Caesar and I had grown close in such a short time—and not even my friendship with Adam could trump that now.

"Watch out. It's hot." Leslie plopped the lasagna onto the table first, then a plate with the baguettes.

Someone walked through the door after we'd all started on the food, and we all froze in sync.

Damian appeared in the doorway, looking a bit ruffled and tired, but okay.

"How is Josh?" Mathilda, who had turned around, gripped the back of her chair.

"Conscious." Damian nodded slightly. Josh had been unconscious through the weekend, intubated—the whole shebang. "Got some problems with his legs, but we hope it's just temporary."

"What problems?" Leslie's eyebrows had drawn together in a frown.

"Paralysis." Damian sighed heavily, dragging a hand through his hair as he did so.

Shit.

"Come eat!" Mathilda jumped up and ran for the counter, where she gathered a plate from the cabinet and cutlery from the drawer. "You need some proper food, and Leslie's made *loads*. It tastes like *heaven*."

My lip tilted up a bit as she used the same description she had earlier. The lasagne sounded, smelled, *and* tasted like heaven. According to her. But it was good, absolutely delicious, to be honest.

Damian sank down heavily on the chair and I could tell he was tired. Exhausted even. He'd stayed with Josh all through the weekend, and those chairs in hospitals weren't made for a good rest.

I wanted to ask questions, wanted to know more about Josh, but Damian looked knackered. And if there were problems… but he *had* said Josh had woken up, which was good. Being conscious was always a good thing.

"Do you think he'll be okay?" Mathilda dared to ask, voice low.

"I don't know." Damian stared down at his plate, but I had a feeling he wasn't exactly seeing it. "I hope so."

Dinner was a tense affair after that. Delicious, but tense. Everyone was worried.

"I'm taking a shower, then I'm going back to the hospital." Damian announced this after everything was cleared off the table and put in the dishwasher.

"Tell Josh we're all thinking about him." It was Leslie who said it, but the rest of us nodded in agreement.

Before Damian could walk off, Mathilda told us she was spending the night with a friend of hers. That would leave me alone in the flat. Just the thought of that made that black hole a little darker, a little more constricting.

"Matt?" Damian cast an askance look at me. He wanted me to be home alone less than I wanted to be home alone.

"I'll stay with Caesar." I'd only left him a little while ago, but he hadn't mentioned any plans for the night. I hoped I was welcome back.

Damian nodded curtly, then walked off to the bathroom.

Mathilda had already disappeared into her room, and now she came back out with a bag thrown over her shoulder. "See you tomorrow." She kissed my cheek, then Adam's, and last Leslie's before breezing out of the flat like she didn't have a care in the world. She was a good pretender, my sister. Strong, fierce, could seem a bit heartless at times—but that was her shield.

My shield was my bed, my duvet over my head. She could just put up a front and live her life, something I felt incapable of managing right now—and had ever since our parents died.

Adam volunteered to do the dishes with me, so Leslie left with a *"See you later, lads"*. We rinsed the dishes and put them in the dishwasher. It didn't take long at all.

"So, you're still seeing that bloke?" Adam bumped my shoulder with his after I shut the dishwasher. "What was his name again?"

"Caesar. Yeah." I felt a flutter in my stomach at the thought of him, like I'd used to get thinking about Adam. I cut my gaze over to him, taking in his profile. He was still exceptionally fine, but so was Caesar. Caesar made me feel happy when otherwise I would be completely miserable. He was attentive, caring—he'd been there for me, while I'd run from him.

I wasn't going to do that again. No way. We were doing this, him and me, this relationship. Trying it out, making it work—and hopefully it would.

"It's serious, then?"

"Yeah." It sure was.

Adam smiled. "That's good. I'm happy for you."

I was quite happy for myself too. Or I would be, if I could get my head on straight. If I could be rid of that never-ending, black hole threatening to consume me. Speaking of that hole... would I ever be rid of it?

I wasn't so sure I would. It seemed like a possibility so far out of reach I couldn't even see it blinking ahead. If I didn't get better than this... what would I do then?

~

Consuming thoughts
Never letting go
Heavy, weighted-down
Grief and guilt combine
To feel better, a blade
across skin
blood drawn
calming down —
then on its heel
shame, regret
They'd never want this
for me
A failure
Scarred
Broken
Lost

I DIDN'T GO to see Caesar. Once Damian left the flat, I went to my bedroom. I curled up in bed with my notebook, and only the light on my bedside table on.

Why didn't I go see him? It was a very good question. I had no answer. I wanted to be alone, but at the same time I didn't. What I desperately needed was my razor blade. It was in my bedside table drawer. Right there, close to me.

Resist it. I couldn't. I hadn't been able to resist in *years*.

My head snapped to the side. I thought I'd seen something move in the shadows, but in sort of a different way than before. But no, I was the only one in my room. In the entire flat. I'd locked the door once I was sure Damian was out of the building. Leaving doors unlocked was not a good idea—that's how, three years ago, Josh's ex-stepfather, Andrew, had got in our house and tried to kill him. It was when Andrew was escaping from it he'd killed Dad. That hadn't been intentional, but that didn't mean I hated him any less.

If he hadn't been so obsessed over Josh, if he hadn't stalked him and tried to kill him when he had the chance… then Dad would be alive. Josh wouldn't have had to be in a coma for days. None of us would have to worry we would attend two funerals, instead of one.

I got the razor blade out of the drawer. There were flecks of blood on it. Dried blood. All mine. Something moved in my peripheral vision again.

There is no one here. If there were, who would it be? I had neither friends nor enemies. The only ones who gave me the time of day were my family, Adam, and Caesar. *Caesar...* I should've gone to stay with him.

My jumper landed in a heap on the floor once I pulled it off and threw it away. My arms still had the stitches in them. I could cut in-between the stitches... or I could start on my upper arms. They were smooth, no damaged skin there.

You'll look like Josh eventually if you start cutting there. What did it matter? I liked the look of Josh's bare arms. All the scars criss-crossing, no smooth skin to be seen... it was fascinating. There was a certain beauty to it—even if what had led to Josh's extensive self-harm was horrible. I'd never experienced any of what he had. The worst thing that had ever happened to me was Dad dying. And Storm... *God, Storm.*

I'd been cutting since before Dad died, though. It was only after he was gone it got more out of hand. That was when I cut deeper. That was when the scars never faded completely once the cuts had healed.

There is someone there! It screamed inside my head

and I jerked back to press my back against the wall. "No. No one's there." *Just my overactive imagination.* All I could see properly though was the edge of my bed, where the razor blade rested in the palm of my hand. Everything else was in shadow, because the blinds were closed and the curtains drawn. Considering my room was painted in a dark colour, all was black outside my little range of light.

I should turn on the overhead light. You can't cross the floor! Why the hell not? It wouldn't take many steps to reach the door and flick the switch. *Don't do it!*

I shook my head, willing the voices away. They didn't go.

My hand shook, and since the blade rested in my palm, so did it. I was drawn to it. It was so small, yet it could cause so much damage. It could cause so much fascination, so much beauty. Cuts, and blood, and scars. They had been an important part of my life for three years.

I'd only started because I'd been curious. I'd been curious about how Josh had felt when *he* started cutting. I could definitely see the addictive effect it had now. I couldn't stop. I didn't *want* to stop.

Something's moving over there. I didn't want to look. I stared at the razor blade instead. *The shadows are moving. No, they're not. Get yourself together. They are moving. The shadows, the posters, the walls...*

No! The blade pressed into my skin, drawing one long line. Blood oozed out. It was even more fascinating to watch blood trickle over the smooth skin than it was over the scarred one. Unharmed skin... it wouldn't be for long. Soon it would have scars as well, just like my forearms.

It would all bleed.

CHAPTER 20

The urge
A craving
Skin crawling with
coming sensation
A blade sliding
over skin
Tingling feeling
of relief
As blood trickle
Staining sheets red

J woke to a door slamming. My phone vibrated next to me. The shadows were still moving, coming closer, circling in around me, suffocating me.

They're going to get you now.

"No, they won't." My arms hurt. Not just my forearm, but the beautiful mess I'd made of both my upper arms as well.

"Matt?"

They're calling for you.

"No, they're not."

No one was calling for me. It was all in my mind, like everything else. It had to be—but I was frozen in terror all the same.

"Matt!"

Go away. Go away. Go away.

There was a knock on the door. *Now they're really coming to get you. There's no way out of this.* There had to be.

"Matt? Are you in?"

"Mathilda?" It had to be her. My mind couldn't be playing this trick on me, could it? Wasn't she spending the night with a friend? Why was she home already? Surely that much time hadn't passed yet.

My door opened. "No, don't come in! They'll get you too!" Even if I was in danger—*was I?*—she didn't have to be. I didn't want her to be.

"What the hell, Matt?"

The light shining through the door, around her, blinded me. I lifted my arm to put it over my eyes, only to have the stitches poke into my skin. That was all it took to get the tears to run and for sobs to erupt from my chest, shaking my whole body.

"Matt?" Mathilda stepped over the threshold and flicked the lights on. "Oh my God, Matt!" She was at my side before I could blink.

I peered up at her through my tears. Though my vision was blurry, I could see her wide eyes and shocked expression. "Where is that thing?" Her eyes narrowed. Now she was angry.

What thing?

"The razor blade! Where is it?"

I shook my head. How should I know? I'd been sleeping before she came barging in the front door, right? Because now I knew *that* sound had been her. It was just everything else that wasn't... "They'll get both of us. You have to go. They're here."

Her eyebrows drew together in confusion. "Who's they?"

"They're here!" I sat up straight, tried to shove her towards the door, but she only stepped out of my range.

"You're covered in blood." She grabbed the back of my neck, the only part that wouldn't result in hurting me. "Get up, Matt. We're going to the bathroom."

"I can't go. They want me here." Her nails were

long and digging into my skin. *Turns out I can hurt in places I hadn't cut, too.*

"Stop it! There's no *they*. Get up, Matt!"

"Oww!" I did rise, simply because her nails really did hurt. My gaze flickered around the room, but there were no shadows now. The overhead light made sure of that. Nothing moved. All was silent, all stayed in place.

"How can you do this to yourself?"

I sank onto the floor once she released me and leaned against the bathtub. There were no shadows in here either. *Good.*

"*This* is no way to deal!" Mathilda held up my razor blade. She must've found it in my bed as she forced me up and out. "You have to *stop*." She stalked over to the toilet, opened the lid, threw the blade in, and flushed it.

"I don't think a razor blade should be flushed in the toilet," was all I managed to say, already mourning the loss of my best friend.

"I'll get rid of it wherever I like to." She turned to me, lips pressed tight, eyes narrowed.

I turned my head away, stared down at my arms instead. The stitches... they were intact, but the blood from my upper arms trickled over them.

"I can't believe you'd do this to yourself." Her voice was strained. The water ran in the sink, then she was at my side, gently pressing a warm, damp cloth to my right arm.

It hurt. I jerked away.

The doorbell rang.

"Bloody hell," Mathilda hissed, pulling the cloth away as she stood up. "I'll be right back. *Don't* do anything stupid."

What stupid things could I do? She'd flushed the razor blade. All I did was rest the side of my head against the bathtub. I even closed my eyes. Tiredness washed over me like a flood, even if I'd just woken a little while ago.

"Hey, Matt…" Mathilda was back.

"Hmm?" My eyes didn't want to open. All I wanted was sleep. I wanted silence, no shadows moving, no voices speaking in my head.

A sharp intake of breath did get my attention. Why had Mathilda brought someone in here? To see me like this…

"Matty?"

Only one person called me that. "Caesar?" I forced my eyes open. He stood there, staring at me over Mathilda's shoulder.

"We have to clean him up," Mathilda said, voice low, teeth biting down on her lower lip. "I don't think he's entirely lucid."

"What do you mean?" Caesar glanced at her.

"I think he's hallucinating."

I'm right here. Don't talk about me like I'm not here. But my vocal chords didn't want to work, didn't want to push the words out.

"Hallucinating what?"

"I don't know. He's just babbling."

I don't babble. And I wasn't hallucinating. Something really is there.

Next thing I knew Caesar's face was right in front of mine. "Hey, Matty. Let's clean you up, okay?"

Mathilda hovered nervously behind him, still biting on her lower lip. "We have to ring someone. He needs help. A lot more help than we can give him."

Caesar cupped my cheek in one palm before he turned to look up at Mathilda. "Can you ring your cousin?"

Mathilda frowned. "He's at the hospital with Josh. I don't know…" She squeezed her eyes shut. "I wish Mum was home."

"No." I finally found my voice. "Don't you dare ring Mum."

"But Matt!" Her eyes brimmed with tears. "She's our mum. She could help."

"Even if she hadn't buggered off with that git, she has no interest in helping me." The bitterness fell out of me before I could stop it. "She's only interested in herself. She sold our house—"

"Because she couldn't afford to keep it on her own!"

"—she killed my dog, she couldn't be arsed with me so she palmed me off on Damian and Josh. She married an arsehole none of us likes, and then she buggered off to the other side of the *world* with him." She wasn't my mum. The Mum I'd known had died the same day Dad had. From that day onwards, everything had truly gone to hell.

"I'm ringing Angelina, then." Mathilda's voice reached a higher pitch. "She always knows what to do."

"Angelina?" Caesar glanced up at her again. His thumb stroked my cheek lovingly.

"She's Josh's mum." Mathilda took her mobile out of her pocket and started pressing her thumb against the screen.

I turned my head away, but regretted it as it also dislodged Caesar's palm against my skin. "Caesar…" I turned back, leant forward, and put my head on his shoulder.

His arms wrapped around my shoulders, holding me tight. "I'm here."

He was. This wasn't a trick of my mind. The feel

of him against me told me loud and clear that he *was* real. "I think I'm going mental."

Caesar didn't say anything to that, just held me close. What could he say, really? It was true.

Mathilda had walked out of the bathroom and I could hear her muffled voice, but I couldn't make out any of the words.

"We need to get you cleaned up, Matty." Caesar pushed me away, back against the tub. "I'll do it, okay?"

My head lolled against the cold edge of the tub. "I'm sorry." He shouldn't have to deal with this. We hadn't known each other for long. We'd only just got *together*.

I heard him move away, heard the tap turn on. But my eyes had closed again and now I couldn't get them to open. If I opened them, I was afraid of what I'd see.

I jerked as a warm, wet cloth pressed against my arm, but then subsided and let Caesar do whatever he wanted.

"Matt?" Mathilda's voice jerked me back into the here and now.

I must've dozed off, because when I pried my eyes open, both Caesar and Mathilda were looking down at me. Caesar had a blood-soaked cloth in his hand—and looking down at myself, I saw that both my arms were bandaged.

"I couldn't get hold of Angelina. She must be at work or with Josh at the hospital. Damian didn't answer either." She chewed her lip nervously.

I rubbed at my eyes. "I'm tired."

Mathilda took the bloody cloth away from Caesar, and he stooped down to help me up on my feet.

"Put him to bed," Mathilda said. "I'll try to get hold of someone again. Someone has to *do* something."

Caesar led me back into my room—and he deposited me on my bed, going so far as to tuck me in. "I'll leave if you want. Or I can wait in the living room with Mathilda?"

Something moved—I could see it in the corner of my eye. "No. Stay. Please." I didn't want to be alone with the shadows. "Don't leave me alone in here." My gaze flickered to the corner, but I couldn't see anything outright. The shadows only moved when my attention wasn't on them.

Caesar followed my gaze.

"I'm scared," I admitted in a low voice.

"I'm here." He climbed onto the bed with me, pushing me in closer to the wall as he stretched out. "Nothing can get you while I'm here."

He was so sweet. Even after seeing the horror of

what I did to myself, he was here with me. "I want to be with you, Caesar." I whispered it against his chest. "I want the label, I want the exclusivity, I want the relationship. I want it with *you*. I want everyone to know that I'm yours and you're mine. That we're together and happily so."

Focusing on him, having my face pressed to his chest and his arm around me, took my mind off the moving shadows. The feel of him, the smell of him, calmed me down a little.

"I want that too, Matty."

"Good." I couldn't even begin to describe just how good it was. "Want to make it official?" I pulled back to look up at him.

He grinned. "With a kiss?"

"That too, but I was thinking more of—" I leant over him to pluck my mobile from my nightstand— careful not to look at the rest of my room as I did so. I unlocked the screen and clicked into my *Facebook* app. I searched him up, found his profile, and pressed *add as friend*.

Caesar's mobile vibrated in his pocket, against our thighs. I fished it out before he could, and since he didn't have a passcode, I clicked right in to confirm the friend request. Then I went back to my own mobile to add us in a relationship. Caesar's mobile vibrated again and I pressed confirm to this request as well.

"We're now officially a couple." I turned both mobiles around to show him. "It's not an official relationship until it's Facebook-official, after all."

He frowned at the screens. "Matthew Fielding is in a relationship with Caesar—" He broke himself off before he could finish the entire sentence as he kissed me—firm, deep, and passionate.

I dropped our mobiles as I kissed him back, loving the feel of his lips against mine. It almost made me forget the looming shadows.

Until Mathilda barged into my room.

"I got hold of Angelina. She's coming over. She's trying to reach Vincent." She clutched her phone tight, gaze going between Caesar and me.

I couldn't meet her gaze, so I moved mine. Something moved in the corner—I knew it did. But they didn't react, so I squeezed my eyes shut so I wouldn't have to see it.

"Matt?" Mathilda's steps were light over the floor. "What's wrong?"

"There's something there." But I refused to open my eyes.

"No, there isn't." She sounded alarmed. "Matt. There isn't anything here. There wasn't earlier, and there isn't now. *Nothing*."

Maybe she was right. But what if she was wrong? I drew in a shaky breath.

"Have you taken anything?" Her voice grew shriller.

"No." I hadn't taken anything. She couldn't blame this on me being on drugs. "There's something *there* and it's out to get me!" And I couldn't bear to look at it, so I turned over to face the wall—only I hit my arm against it and cried out.

"Hey, shhh." Caesar stroked my back. It was supposed to be soothing, but it *wasn't*.

Tears leaked from my eyes. "I don't want to live like this." I didn't want to live with the pain, with the depression, with the worry, with being scared of my own bloody room. "I don't want to!" My body trembled as I sobbed into my pillow.

"Matt—"

The doorbell rang, shutting Mathilda up. She left my room in a hurry and I heard muffled voices as she answered the door.

Caesar moved away from me. *Maybe he's already had enough.* I couldn't blame him.

"Come on, Matthew." Strong, sure arms grabbed my shoulders. "You're coming with me to A&E." I let Angelina turn me around and push me up into a sitting position. She took in my bandaged arms, the blood soaking my sheets and clothes, with a face that betrayed nothing. *But then she's used to this from Josh, isn't she?*

It only made me sob harder. And when I dared a peak around the room, and once again saw something move, I curled up on myself. "No, no, *no!*" I didn't want to see those things, whatever they were. I didn't want to me a cried out, cut up mess.

"Matthew." Angelina wrestled me out of bed and up on my feet. Other hands grabbed at me now too… Caesar's. "Let's get you to hospital."

Hospital. That's where Damian was. That's where *Josh* was. "Josh?" I managed to get out, my mind a jumbled mess.

"He's been moved to a locked ward. But physically, he'll be fine." Angelina delivered this new in a short, clipped tone.

That's good. Except if Josh had been put in a locked ward, he'd be away for a while. Right? And what if I got to the hospital and was sectioned? Would they do that? If they did, Damian would be all alone… Once Mum came home, Mathilda would move back in with her.

Caesar's arm wrapped around my waist, pulling me in close. My arm flashed with pain, but I ignored it as I leaned in against him.

"Come on, Matthew. You need to get your arms looked at." Angelina steered me—us, since I was attached to Caesar now—towards the door. I got my legs moving, eager to be out of my dark bedroom. "Vincent will meet us there."

Vincent... I'd only ever been to that one session with him. I had no idea what he'd thought about me afterwards, but now he'd get it confirmed. That I really was mentally ill.

Tears streamed down my cheeks, but the sobs had stopped. My breathing was a bit erratic, but that was all the sound that left me.

"You'll get through this, Matthew." Angelina squeezed my shoulder. "We'll get you help now. It'll be better soon."

I could only hope soon would come around pretty quickly.

CHAPTER 21

*B*eing in hospital was nothing like I'd thought it would be. Not that I'd imagined anything in particular, but... They were gentle with me, but firm. They were cautious about the medication they administered, but clear on the fact I had to take what the doctor prescribed.

I was in a psychosis and they had to administer antipsychotics to get it under control. Maybe the pills made the shadows stop moving or maybe it was the fact they left me so drowsy that did it... but it did help.

By the fourth day, I was up and moving. At least I went out to have breakfast. Because I'd agreed to be admitted to a psychiatric ward, I hadn't been sectioned. *Thank fuck*. This also meant I wasn't on a locked ward like him.

I could, technically, leave if I wanted to. But what did I have to go home too? More of the same of this? Self-harm and moving shadows and scary voices... no, better to stay and get help and be able to leave saner than I came in.

"You've got visitors, Matt," a nurse told me later that day.

It was Damian and Mathilda. Mathilda ran towards me when I entered the room, throwing herself around my neck and hugging me so tight I might just suffocate. Damian stood back and regarded me silently.

"How are you?" Mathilda asked, voice strained. "We weren't allowed to see you the last three days, they say you haven't been well enough. Are you now? Are you getting better?"

"It takes longer than four days, Mathilda," Damian reminded her quietly.

"The treatment's working a little, I think," I mumbled, slinking further into the room as she released me.

Mathilda sank onto the sofa, biting her lip nervously as she grabbed her bag and started rifling through it. "I brought some stuff for you. Your note-book, the one you're always writing in—" She saw the look I gave her and held her hands up. "Don't worry, I haven't looked in it. But it was on your bedside table so I thought you'd like it."

"Josh likes to have something near for writing," Damian supplied quietly.

I looked at him. "How is Josh?"

"We're still not allowed in to see him."

Shit. What did that mean? I was afraid to ask.

Maybe Damian saw something on my face, because he said, "He's not cooperating. That makes it more difficult."

What did *that* mean? He didn't leave me any less confused. Not cooperating? Didn't Josh want to take the medication they prescribed for him? Didn't he want to go to therapy? Or to breakfast? Was he *violent?* I couldn't picture Josh being violent, though. He was a bundle of nerves if anything. Worse than me.

"You think I have to stay long?" I asked, bowing my head over the notebook I'd taken from Mathilda. I hoped she'd been sincere when she said she hadn't looked inside it—hadn't seen all my awful poems.

"Hard to say," Damian said. "It all depends on you, if you cooperate, if you respond to medication and therapy. You could be out quickly, or… you could stay a while."

Fuck. "What about Caesar?"

"He came with us yesterday," Mathilda said, "but he had to work today."

Yesterday... Damn it. Why'd I have to stay knocked out from the medication during visiting hours? I could've seen him, hugged him, but no... instead I'd been slumped miserably in bed. It wasn't even a very comfortable bed. "I'm so tired. It's the medicine, I think..." I rubbed at my eyes.

"Give it time," Damian cautioned. "Meds need time to work. And if it doesn't get better, they'll try you on other sorts of medicine. Until they find one that works without adverse side effects, they'll keep trying."

That made me sound like a guinea pig.

"No one's the same," Daman continued, like he'd read my mind. "An antipsychotic that works for one person doesn't necessarily work for another."

I stared glumly at the floor. "Why can't it just work right away? I hate feeling like this." The hallucinations were gone, or whatever it had been, but feeling so drained and tired all the time... I didn't want to be so damn miserable.

"It'll get better." Damian sounded reassuring. Then again, he'd been through this before, several times, with Josh. But just look at where Josh was now... back in hospital, in a locked ward. That's where he always ended up, wasn't it?

"Why're you crying?" Mathilda asked, shooting to her feet so she could stand in front of me.

"I—" I touched my cheeks and indeed… I was crying. "I don't want to be like this. I don't want to end up in hospital time and time again." *Like Josh…* I couldn't say it though, because Damian was here and he loved Josh so much and it must be unbearable for him that he'd almost lost him again.

Mathilda wrapped an arm around my shoulders. "Feeling like that is good, right? You want to change… so you will. You just need to find what works best for you in terms of medication and therapy."

I doubted it was that easy, but it was a little reassuring to hear. And anyway, I had them in my corner no matter what. Josh, too, when he was well.

"Matt?" Mathilda's unsure voice broke into my thoughts.

"Mmm?"

"Mum wants to come see you." She stared into my eyes, gauging my reaction.

"No," I said, not even thinking about it. "I don't want her visiting me."

"But she's worried about you. She really wants to see you."

"No way." If she was so worried, she should've done something sooner instead of palming me off on

Damian and Josh. She should've seen I wasn't doing so well—she could've kept Storm alive or not replaced Dad the minute his grave had sunk.

But she'd made her decisions. And I'd made mine. "If she comes here, I'll just tell the staff I don't want to see her, and they'll listen to me. I'm allowed to decide who I want to see or not." Mum couldn't force her presence on me no matter what.

Mathilda bit her lip.

"Can you bring Caesar with you this weekend?" I wasn't sure if he worked, but even if he worked tomorrow, he always had Sundays off. "I want to see him."

"Of course." This was Damian.

"He was bummed we didn't get to see you yesterday." Mathilda squeezed my shoulder reassuringly. "He really likes you." She sounded almost *approving* for a change.

"So do you like him?" I asked, but I didn't dare look at her to see her reaction.

"He's grown on me," was all she said, but I could hear the smile in her voice. "Anyway, besides that notebook, I also brought some pens for you." She turned back to her bag and pulled out three, all in different colours; black, blue, and red. "I wasn't sure which one you like best and since all three of them were on your bedside table I figured I'd play it safe."

"Thanks." I took them from her, clenching my fist around them. I'd have something to do in here now; that was good. Instead of lying listlessly in bed or staring at the wall or mingling with the rest of the crazy people. Of which I was one, but still. Why make friends in a psychiatric hospital when I wasn't likely to ever meet them again?

Mathilda hugged me again. It was getting weird, but she didn't seem to want to stop. "Don't fucking scare me like that again, okay?" she said then, voice low, lips against my ear. "I can't lose you too, you hear me? None of us can."

I swallowed the lump that instantly stuck in my throat. Or tried anyway. It wasn't budging. "I'll try."

She sighed, slumping against me. "That's all I can ask for, I guess."

"I'll try my best." It was certainly all I could give.

∾

Death
Never-ending
Forever
Alone
With secrets
Never told
Guilt

> *gnawing*
> *never letting go*
> *A wish*
> *to say the words*
> *never told*

WHEN I LATER SAT CROSS-LEGGED on my bed, with my notebook open to the last poem I'd written, pen pointed over the next blank page, poised to write... I couldn't come up with any dreadful poetry.

All I could think about was Caesar and what a whirlwind romance—could it be called a romance, really?—we'd had. What I wanted to be at home doing to him now instead of being stuck in a psychiatric hospital.

The pen hovered over the first line, words forming in my head. They weren't the literary kind of words that Josh was good at—he wrote books with deeper meaning, usually taken from his own horrible childhood. The words forming in my mind were, basically porn.

But hell, someone had to write the porn too, right? And it wasn't like anyone would ever see this. Well, except maybe Caesar—he'd find it hot. Maybe I'd get to do all the things I thought about to him when I was finally out of here.

The first sentence came easily. The second one too. And the third.

This is much better than writing shitty poetry. Writing porn instead. Hell, who would've thought? Maybe this was what I was meant to do instead of agonising over poetry; write filthy smut for only my boyfriend's eyes. We could act it out too, as Caesar was pretty open when it came to sex.

I didn't think he'd mind being written into a porn story at all. He'd find it hilarious and hot and he'd actually *want to* re-enact it in real life.

That's Caesar for you, yeah.

It was like the pen flew over the lines, writing every single word that tumbled into my brain. I had no idea where they even came from, as I'd never had an inkling about writing anything but poems before.

Yet here I was, half way down my first page of an actual story. Not that it had a plot—which teachers at school had always drilled into the pupils a story needed. It didn't need a plot. It needed for the main characters to get off. That was the all-important goal of the story and I was damn well going to get them there… after torturing them for a bit.

I walked out of the psychiatric hospital to a bright, sunny afternoon. Damian walked at my side, my bag slung over one shoulder.

His face was an expressionless mask, but that was nothing new. I knew he was doing okay, though, especially as I saw Josh push away from the hood of his mother's car.

"Matt!" Josh smiled wide as he came over to me, and his arms wrapped around me in a hug. He'd only been to see me the day before yesterday, but it felt a lot longer than that. I clutched at him in return.

My gaze travelled over Josh's shoulder, taking in the other two people leaning against the car. Mathilda detached herself now, coming over to hug both me and Josh.

Behind them was Caesar, devoid of his fashion-able glasses today, as he gazed at me with a bit of worry, a bit of excitement.

I pulled back from the hugs, brushed around Mathilda, and headed straight for Caesar. I hadn't seen him in *days*. That was too long.

"Hey, Matty." He opened his arms and I stepped right into them. "It's so good to see you again."

I'd been in hospital for three weeks and two days, and though Caesar had been to see me regularly, he hadn't been able to see me as often as my family, because his job always tended to clash with visiting hours.

"I'm so glad you're here." I never thought I'd be so relieved to hug someone close as I was right now.

"How are you feeling?" Caesar drew back to look at me, gaze searching mine.

"I'm good." And I was. After the first week, which had been really bad, I'd done better and better. "Got a whole lot of drugs to take from now on though." They'd put me on antidepressants and antipsychotics—a different one than they'd first put me on, as that had left me too sleepy to function much. My preliminary diagnosis as of now was psychotic depression.

Caesar chuckled. "That makes two of us. I reckon we have to be careful not to mix our drugs, then."

"Yeah." I stared into his blue eyes, mesmerised by them. "I don't think antipsychotics will do much for you. Nor will anticonvulsants do much for me."

I was far from done with treatment. I was only trying out my medication for now—I might have to end up having to change it down the line if it didn't work properly or if the side effects were too much to handle.

But as of right now, I felt good. Better than I had in a while. But being back in Caesar's arms, knowing that I was going home, that I could finally be with him again… that was what made me feel great.

Damian got into the driver's seat, on the other side of the car from us. Mathilda slid into the back-seat, whereas Josh took the passenger seat in front. I fumbled for the door-handle and slid in to sit in-between Mathilda and Caesar.

Caesar took my hand in his once we'd both secured our seat belts. He laced our fingers together in a silent show of affection. My heart soared.

"Where to now?" Damian looked at me in the mirror as he started the car.

I didn't need to think about it. I'd made my decision before I'd even left the hospital. "The cemetery."

They all threw me startled glances.

"There's someone I want Caesar to meet."

∾

I WRAPPED my arms around myself as I stopped in front of the grave. Caesar stood shoulder-to-shoulder with me, gazing down at the stone.

"I can't even imagine what it must be like to lose a parent." He bit his lower lip.

I crouched down to run my fingers over the gold inscription on my dad's stone. "Dad." My voice was low. It felt a bit silly talking to a grave, considering the person in it couldn't ever answer me, but I needed to do this. "It's Matt. I've brought someone with me to meet you."

Caesar slowly crouched down next to me.

"This is Caesar. My boyfriend." I bumped our shoulders. "I wish you could've met him. He's wonderful."

Caesar looked at me. "I wish I could've met him too."

"He would've liked you." I smiled, knowing that my words were the truth. Dad would've accepted Caesar just as easily as he'd always accepted Josh. As he'd accepted everyone. My parents had been easy-going, never speaking ill of anyone.

Except Mum had changed now. But I wasn't here to think about her—or the tosser she'd married. It felt like she was betraying Dad.

Caesar's hand found mine and squeezed. "I'm sure I would've liked him too."

I leaned into him, resting my head on his shoulder. "I think Dad would've been happy for me. Happy that I've found someone I like. Someone like you."

"I'm hardly anything to brag about." That was an uncharacteristically meek remark, coming from him.

"*I* seem to remember a *lot* of bragging on your part." I couldn't help but tease. It wasn't untrue, after all. I could clearly remember something about him promising to fuck me until I saw stars.

"Okay, so maybe I'm a great catch. You really couldn't have done any better." He grinned wickedly, eyes alight.

I smiled back. "You're entirely too confident in yourself."

"It's entirely a facade, I tell you."

I grinned wider. It might be true when it came to other people, but not to me. To me, Caesar was perfect. He could be as confident and bragging as he wanted to around me, because he was simply a piece of perfection.

"You're a dork." I chuckled as I lifted my head from his shoulder to bend in closer to him.

He only laughed and pulled me in close by the

front of my jacket. I moaned softly as our lips meshed together.

I was sure I'd discover some not-so-good sides to him in time, when we knew each other better, but as for now… we were new, exciting, he made me feel alive again. He made me smile, laugh when nothing else could.

One thing I hoped was that I'd never get tired of this. Never get tired of him. Because with him I felt alive—and I didn't ever want to lose that. Not the feeling, not him, not what we'd just started.

We were young. There were no guarantees for our future… but I had hope.

And really, that was all I needed.

"So what now?" Caesar asked. "Are you coming back to my flat with me?"

Considering Damian had dropped off us and I'd told him not to wait, that was a moot question. Then again… "Just for today? Or to stay?"

A grin spread slowly on his lips. "Whatever you want, Matty. I've been waiting three weeks for you to get out of hospital. If it were up to me, I wouldn't let you leave my place ever again."

A laugh bubbled out of me. It felt incredible to laugh again. I hadn't felt happy in so long. Maybe my medicines were working, maybe my period of depression was over, or maybe it was a placebo effect... whatever it was, for now I felt *good*.

"You'll get sick of me," I teased, but it held a sliver of truth.

"We'll work it out." He, on the hand, was so confident. "If we fight, we'll have the most amazing make-up sex." He kissed me again, deeper this time.

I could certainly believe that. Sex with Caesar *was* amazing. I didn't have much to compare it too—but I didn't need to. I'd always thought of myself as someone who preferred to top, but after Caesar... it felt so natural and so fantastic to have him top *me*. I didn't want it any other way.

I slid my lips against his in a feather-light kiss. "How about some welcome-home sex?"

He laughed out loud, eyes twinkling as he looked at me. "I like the sound of that. And after that, let's get to some of those stories you told me about. Something about re-enacting them?"

A startled laugh left me. "Yeah, let's get to that, too."

I gazed at Dad's grave one last time before I let Caesar pull me up onto my feet. I wasn't dumb enough to think that everything would be all fine and dandy after three weeks in hospital. Having now had one psychotic episode, they were much more likely to happen again if I got depressed. And they would —I was sure of it.

But I had an initial diagnosis, so I knew what I was dealing with. I had medicine that seemed to work right now. I had Damian, and Josh, and Mathilda... and best of all, I had a boyfriend. I had Caesar.

What more could I ask for?

TT lives in Norway and writes about gay men living in Norway. She also occasionally writes about gay men living in the UK, because she loves the UK. Norway might be too cold for her, but TT doesn't like the summer, so she's learned to adapt. TT is happiest in front of her computer, creating emotional stories about men loving other men.

www.ttkove.com
ttkove@gmail.com